Loving on the edge

A Story of Forbidden Love in the Church

BY EWAN DENNY

MINISTRY IN ART PUBLISHING
communicating excellence

Ministry In Art Publishing Ltd
email: publishing@ministryinart.com
website: miapublishing.com

This publication is designed to provide accurate and authoritative information in regard to the subject matter covered. It is sold with the understanding that the publisher is not engaged in rendering legal, accounting, or other professional service. If legal advice or other expert assistance is required, the services of a competent professional should be sought.

ISBN: 978-0-9551496-7-2

Cover design by Allan Sealy
www.miadesign.com

Table of Contents

Acknowledgements

To my wife Jennifer who never ceases to amaze me and to whom I owe the greatest of respect for the joy that she has brought into my life.

To my first and blessed god-son David whom I shall meet again one day.

Important Note

None of the characters in this book are based on real persons but are derived purely from the imagination of the Author.

About the Author

Ewan Denny is a christian marketing and communications specialist who has dedicated himself to applying powerful marketing techniques within the context and guidelines of the scriptures, to present Jesus Christ to the world as Lord and Saviour, and to help fellow christians and churches everywhere to do the same. He has been a Christian since 1979.

Educated to post-graduate level in marketing management at Leeds Metropolitan University, Ewan has been the Head of Marketing and Communications for a range of colleges, public sector bodies, and private companies. He now runs his own marketing consultancy practice in London and is also a professional Business Coach.

He is also a freelance journalist and has written and produced a number of books, publications and audio programmes on business, marketing and biblical subjects.

Ewan's particular joy is to help churches to market themselves better and to promote Jesus Christ in the most effective way, and this led him to Author his first book "The Marketing of Jesus Christ."

Ewan helps churches to enhance their profile and reputation in their areas, and to increase their membership. He believes that the salvation of souls is precious and what churches ought to be doing is to effectively preach the Gospel in order to save souls and to prepare them for the second coming of Christ. He believes that good marketing and communications has a major role to play in this and in the preaching of the Gospel.

Telephone: +44 (0) 7962 630 724
Email: info@ewandenny.com
Website: www.ewandenny.com

Chapter 1

It is a hot Saturday evening in July and the church is packed. It's the last night of a week long thanksgiving service to celebrate the church's "coming of age." Mount Zion Refuge, based in Old Trafford, Manchester, is 18 years old, having grown from just 26 people when it started, to now over 5000. The building is quite old but newly refurbished and is very comfortable.

"We shall have a grand time, up in heaven" the church is singing, "we shall have a grand time up in heaven, have a grand time, talking with the angels, singing glory hallelujah, we shall have a grand time up in heaven, have a grand time."

Most people are on their feet singing, clapping, bodies swaying, faces enlightened. The musicians are in their zone, playing with skill, though many of the older brethren think that they are playing too loud.

This has certainly been a blessed week. Though blessed, it has also been tiring. Mothers have been in the kitchen cooking the food that is served after each service. They have missed most of the services even though there is a rota, but they are happy about doing service for the Lord. A loudspeaker is placed in the kitchen so that they can hear what is going on, but it is not the same. Nevertheless, they are happy. And tired. Some complain about aching feet.

A few squabbles broke out in the heat of the kitchen but nothing serious.

In the congregation, little children are getting restless. They keep pretending that they are going to the toilet (so that their parents don't tell them to sit down), but once outside, they play and have some fun with their friends.

It's very hot inside the building. People are sweating. The ceiling fans are on but it just seems to be blowing hot air. The singing is finished. Everyone sits down. Hand held fans are seen all over the place. It's time for the preacher.

"Brethren" announces Peter Thompson, the Moderator who is leading the service, "thank God for that song. It always reminds me that this race is not in vain, but we are all running for a prize." The church shouts a loud "Amen."

"The Bible says that the race is not for the swift, neither the battle for the strong, but it is for he that endureth to the end. When we sing about having a grand time up in heaven, we are reminding ourselves of this spiritual journey that will end in heaven, if we continue in the faith, and if we faint not."

Peter continues to speak along these lines but whilst no-one can disagree with what he is saying, many are getting annoyed that he is still speaking. "Why can't he just shut up now and hand the service over to Pastor" one sister says. "He just likes the sound of his own voice."

Peter, who is also the Choir Leader, is an ambitious young man and he never gives ten words when a hundred will do. "I keep my body under subjection" he continues, totally unaware of the body language of the congregation which is begging him to sit down. "I don't want that after all that I have done, I hear depart from me I know you not. I want to make it home." As he says this a voice is heard in the background "and we want you to make it to your chair now."

Some people start to laugh. Embarrassed and not knowing who made the comment, Peter is thrown off his stride and forgets what point he was making. Thinking quickly, he says, "brethren, its time for the Word. On this Saturday night, the last day of the feast, we believe that the Lord has something in store for us. Let's stand on our feet in respect to the man of god that will be coming to us. Church put your hands together for Pastor Joseph Ellington."

Over 5,000 pairs of hands start to clap at the same time. The noise is deafening. Pastor Ellington is very much respected in Mount Zion Refuge. His personal standing with the saints is very high. Married with four children, this 52 year old well built man dressed in a sharp navy blue suit, white shirt and red tie, comes to the podium.

"Brethren, help me to sing this song" says Pastor, "It's one of my favourites." The congregation rises, and with songbooks in hand, they begin to sing:

The church is one foundation,
Is Jesus Christ her Lord.
She is His new creation
By water and the Word.
From heaven He came and sought her
To be His holy bride;
With His own blood He bought her
And for her life He died.

All together, the voices sing out. People are standing at the back because there are not enough seats for everyone. Some are outside the hall, unable to get in. Busy Ushers are working overtime to keep some sort of order as people who leave their seats to go to the toilet, return to find that their seats are taken by other people. Some give up the seat when spoken to but others refuse to move. "There was nobody sitting here. I am not moving now." They say bluntly.

The church continues to sing:

Mid toil and tribulation,
And tumult of her war,

She waits the consummation
Of peace forevermore;
Till, with the vision glorious,
Her longing eyes are blest,
And the great Church victorious
Shall be the Church at rest.

The song finishes and everyone sits down, waiting to hear from the Pastor. "Tonight is a very special night" he begins. "When the Lord was calling me to be the Pastor of this church, I did not want to do it. I was a bit like Jonah trying to escape to Tarshish. I just did not want to Pastor people because of all the trouble that it brings. People always think that it is easy to be a Pastor. They think that all we do is to come up here and preach. No my friend, the job of Pastor is very stressful, very demanding and very trying. Leading people in business, at work, or in the church, is very difficult.

I went in prayer to the Lord and gave Him my excuses as to why I could not be the Pastor. The Lord listened, but said nothing. I kept on praying and talking to God about it. Again, the Lord said nothing. Finally, after a few days, I got a bit annoyed and pleaded with God and asked Him again to choose somebody else. I waited for an answer. I said speak Lord, thy servant heareth. I waited and waited, and I then heard a voice that said to me "do what I have told you to do."

And that was it. It was not the answer that I wanted

to hear. The Lord did not respond to my reasoning and my excuses about not being able to do the job of a Pastor. He ignored it all and told me what He already told me. I could not do anything but say yes Lord. And from a simple beginning with a few people, the church has grown to over 5000 members. Today we are celebrating 18 years as a church and for that I want to say thank you Lord. God knows what He is doing. All we have to do is to bow to His greater will and purpose and allow Him to lead us. Even if we think that another way is better. The Lord knows best."

Shouts of "hallelujah" begin to ring out all over the congregation. "Today we are 18. The church has come of age. We are mature. Let us behave as mature children of God. Let our godliness appear to all men. Let them see Christ fully formed in us. Let us not think and behave like children any more. We are grown up now."

For the next fifty minutes, Pastor Ellington preached a message about living a mature life in Christ, exhorting the church to live up to the godly standards that are outlined in the Bible. The saints gave him audible backing with lots of "Amen"s and "praise the Lord"s.

"We must be like Peter and John" Pastor told the people. "When the lame man begged them for alms one day at the Gate Beautiful, they said "Look on us" and as the man did so anticipating some money, Peter said, "silver and gold have I none, but such as I have give I unto thee, in the name of Jesus Christ, rise up and walk." Then Peter took him by the hand and he got up, his feet and ankle bones received strength and he began to jump up into the air and praising god. We might not have the riches of this world, but we have something inside of us that is far more valuable – we have Christ. We have riches that the world does not know about, and through our lives, we can be a blessing to others. We can make a difference in their lives."

Pastor Ellington concluded his message with an altar call and asked everyone to hold hands and look to the Lord for another year of blessing, and for strength to continue to fight the good fight of faith.

At the end of the service, when everyone was greeting each other, a strong feeling of fellowship and unity permeated the atmosphere. Lots of hugs and handshakes with smiling faces could be seen all over the place. A look of satisfaction could be seen on Pastor Ellington's face as he stood on the platform looking down at the saints greeting each other.

"Thank god for all this" says Mother Ellington, his immaculately dressed wife, who walks up to him and wraps her arms around his waist. "Yes" he replies, "if it was not for the Lord that was on our side, where would we be?"

The following day was Sunday. Church again. Many

of the speakers spoke about the blessings of the Convocation and Pastor paid a special tribute to all the workers who made the entire week so successful – the cooks, the Ushers, the cleaners, the musicians, the choir, the car park attendants and the servers.

After the morning service, everyone went home for dinner. Because the church had been out all week, Sunday night's meeting was cancelled so that the saints could get some rest before going off to work on Monday morning.

At the Pastor's home

Around the dining table in the Ellington home, Pastor and his 3 children (who were still at home) were seated and talking about the West Indies cricket team and whether or not they will ever regain their position as the worlds best. The fourth child, Joel, the eldest, no longer lives at home. He left when he was just 19 after some arguments and frustration with church life.

Mother Ellington, comes into the expensive looking dining room with a large tray on which is a huge roast chicken with roast potatoes and fried plantain around the sides.

"Yes man, I have been waiting for this" declares David, age 17, the youngest child, sporting his Manchester United cap. Still in college and half way through his A'Levels, David is a bright young man and is working towards being an architect.

"Ok David, we are about to eat, you can take that cap off now" says Dawn, his elder sister by three years. David looks at her, but says nothing, and removes his cap. More food is brought out. Father says grace and everyone starts to eat.

"You are quiet today" says Pastor Ellington to Jackie, his eldest daughter, a very beautiful young woman with spotless skin, black flowing hair and a slim, model like figure. "I am fine" she answers. "Come on, something is bothering you. I can always tell. What's on your mind darling?"
"It's just something at work dad" she replies.
"You've got problems?"

"No, not me, but the company has. We were all told on Friday to come for a special staff meeting with the Chairman on Monday morning because he has some important news for us. Everyone is saying that because profits have gone down since we lost two major contracts this year, that redundancies are going to take place. We don't know what is going to happen."
"You didn't mention any of this before!"
"No, it was in the middle of convocation and I didn't want to think about it. We'll see what happens tomorrow."

The Ellington family is a strong one. They are closely knit. Joel, the eldest, is now 25. He left home at age 19 in angry circumstances having fallen out with church life. He was once saved but is now backslidden. Joel found it very difficult being the son of a preacher and felt that he could not live up to the high standards that were expected of him. The mental pressure of always having to be perfect was sometimes too strenuous and difficult to cope with. He was always into health and fitness and he played many sports. Some of the brethren made comments about him being "too carnal" because of this and said that he should be engaged in more "spiritual" activities.

In frustration at hearing these comments over and over again, Joel pointed out some of their carnal ways and highlighted certain behaviours and mistakes that they had made, and said that these were far worse than him playing a sport. This caused major problems as his critics, who were invariably much older than him, complained to his father, the Pastor, saying that this young man was going around talking their business and being rude.

Pastor Ellington, appeased the older women by speaking harshly to his son and saying that he must not talk to the older mothers in the church like that. Joel was made to apologise and by the way he did it, Pastor received more complaints.

He called Joel and said angrily that they had told him that he came into the room and said "Pastor has told me that I must apologise. So I apologise." They felt that he said this with an attitude and that he was not really apologising but simply obeying instructions and had no remorse. Joel called them hypocrites and fell out with his father over the matter. "You always take the side of everyone in church against me" he said. "That's not true" replied his father, and the two battled it out for twenty minutes before Joel stormed off in a huff.

The following week, Joel moved out of the house. He is now living with Eve, his girlfriend. They have a two year old son called Ramone. They don't go to church as Joel does not want to go to any church any more.

The Ellington family tuck into their meal and share some jokes around the table. They tease each other and bring up several family secrets that others outside the family do not know. David, the youngest, likes to especially tease Jackie because everyone thinks that she is "miss goody two shoes" and is just perfect. Because David lives with her, he knows her little mannerisms and bad habits and he finds this contrast hilarious.

Jackie takes it all in good humour and gives back as good as she gets. Many brothers in church find her very attractive but they are afraid to approach her because she is the Pastor's daughter. They are scared of the prospect of having to be whiter than white and perfect in every way in order to get the blessing of Pastor for his daughter. Two brothers in the past three years have tried however, but it didn't work out. The first was told a straight "No" by Jackie because he was too immature. He approached her with some foolish chat up lines and lost any chance that he might have had.

The second brother got a bit further and Jackie was interested initially, that is until she found out that he had asked two other sisters in the church to marry him and they had refused. She was insulted that she was third choice and blew him out with contempt. Jackie feels that she is a princess and is a golden prize for any man who must love her deeply for who she is. And love only her! At age 23, Jackie has thought about marriage but with no one in sight, she is concentrating on serving the Lord and being the best christian that she can be.

The Ellington family finish their meal and recline to the lounge. David remains in the dining room to clear up with Dawn. Pastor and Mother Ellington are holding hands and snuggling up to each other on the sofa, whilst Jackie is watching the Discovery Channel on TV.

At Jackie's workplace

Mr Carson, the Chairman of Carson's Printing, has just finished delivering his speech about hard times and company performance over the last two quarters. He is talking over the heads of most people but the message is loud and clear – the company is in trouble and has to shed some of its staff in order to bring the books back into line. This means seven redundancies.

No-one is clear as to whose jobs will be lost so everyone is nervous.

Jackie works in the marketing department and whilst slightly troubled, she believes that the company cannot cut marketing as it's such an important business function, especially as the company needs to market itself even more now, and try to win new business. The Chairman announces that he will be speaking with the managers and will be making a decision within the next 48 hours.

Jackie has not been out of a job since leaving school. A hard worker, she decided that university was not for her as it was too academic. So after successfully completing her 3 A'Levels, she got an administrative job which she held for three years before moving on to Carson's Printing for the past two years. She enjoys marketing and hopes to make this her chosen career. She is currently taking a Chartered Institute of Marketing course in marketing management and is already an Affiliate member of the organisation.

Two days later, at 11am on Wednesday morning, Mr Carson, the Chairman, is back addressing the workforce. "It is with great regret" he began by saying, "that I have the unpleasant task of informing you who will be made redundant from the company." He then went on to say how much he has valued the contributions that these seven people have made and that this decision has been a hard one and that it is no reflection on the individuals concerned. He then read out the list of names, from one to six and listed the departments that they had been working in. He then said "and the final person ... is Jackie Ellington from Marketing."

Jackie shrieked. "I cannot believe it" she murmured. Mr Carson announced that the unfortunate seven will receive good references, and will have a week's notice. Other workers will be reorganised so that the business could meet all its obligations and fulfil its contracts.

At the Pastor's house

Pastor Ellington is in a counselling session in his private study. Before him are Sister Brenda and Brother John. The two have been married for 18 months now and are having problems. Brother John is accusing his wife of unbearable jealousy and a lack of trust in him. "Pastor, she goes behind my back and checks my text messages, who I ring and who rings me. She even listens into my conversations. I can't stand it any more."

Sister Brenda does not deny checking his messages but says that she does not listen in on his telephone conversations. After much discussion, Brenda declares that it is because other sisters in church like him and he seems so friendly towards them, that makes her so suspicious. She feels that they are flirting with him and trying to entice him but that he does not recognise it. She has mentioned it to him a few times and he says that she is being paranoid. "A woman knows these things" she replies but he just thinks that they are simply being friendly and he is only saying hello.

Whilst Pastor is dealing with the situation, in another area of the house, Jackie arrives home and finds her mother in the kitchen. "Mum, I have been made redundant" she says bursting into tears. "Oh no" Mother Ellington replies and hugs her. The two talk for a while and Mother Ellington reassures her that all will be well, that she will soon find another job and maybe an even better one, paying more money.

"Where's dad?" Jackie asks. Her mother tells her that he is in the study with some brethren and that he should be done soon.

Two hours later, Pastor Ellington comes out of his study and goes out of the house to see another member of the church who is having financial problems in his business and is facing bankruptcy. Jackie has been going up to the door of his study every now and then to see if the meeting was still taking place, but this time, the door is open and Pastor is nowhere to be seen. He has left the house. She retires to her room saying to herself that when she really needs her father, he is often too busy being the Pastor and dealing with everyone else.

There have been many occasions that Jackie and the other children have experienced these feelings. They know that their father loves them and that he has a lot of responsibility as the Pastor, but sometimes they just want him to be dad. They wish that he was at home more, spending quality time with them.

The following day at Carson's Printing, Jackie is speaking with Paul McKenzie, one of the seven people being made redundant. He works in the IT department and is distraught that he is losing his job after he gave so much to the company. Paul is white, 26 years of age, and this has been his only job since coming out of university. He never spoke to Jackie much before, only the occasional hello at the photocopier, but now, facing the same redundancy situation, they have something in common and are talking over lunch, outside of the company.

They speak about what has happened and why they think that they were chosen out of 23 people in the firm. Jackie has some major credit card issues and has not told her parents about it, whilst Paul, an only child, lives alone with his mother, and she has a cleaning job which does not pay very much. He in effect, is the breadwinner in the home.
His father left after a bitter divorce many years ago, when he was just 9.

Over the course of the next week, Paul and Jackie continue speaking and encouraging each other. They are both job hunting and keeping an eye out for suitable jobs for each other. When the week is over, they leave Caron's Printing and say goodbye.

Pastor Ellington knows about Jackie's redundancy and is encouraging her to trust the Lord for something better. He has been out of the home most evenings this week and has not been very accessible to his children. He is mostly coming from or going to a meeting to do with church business. Jackie does not speak with him about what's troubling her, as he seems so busy. She really would like the time to sit quietly and talk with him but feels left out of his busy schedule. "The church always comes first" she says to herself, "and that's the way it is."

That evening, Jackie receives a call from Paul who says that he has seen a job advert for a company that is looking for IT people and someone to work in marketing. They agree to meet up the following day to go to the company. They do so, fill in application forms and a few days later, are both selected for interview. Paul is interviewed first at 11.30am for his IT role and Jackie is seen at 2.30pm. Upon leaving her interview, she walks through Reception and sees Paul seated, reading a magazine.

"I thought your interview was this morning?" she says, surprised to see him.
"Yes it was, but I came back to wait for you.
How was the interview?
"It was OK. But it's difficult to judge."

The two of them go to a nearby café to talk. They share things about each other, and are open and honest about their feelings. Paul fancies Jackie but she does not know it. To her, they are just friends who have come together by act of fortune, out of a bad situation, and they have something in common.

They both feel that they can talk and confide in each other because they are both from different worlds and are outside of each other's social networks, so there is no pretence or having to keep up a certain image. They enjoy open and honest conversations, and neither are judgemental of the other.

As time passes, they keep in touch more regularly. Paul was successful in his job application and has already started with the company. Jackie is still looking and all the while becoming more desperate as the 3 credit card companies are regularly calling her about her overdue balances. She does not know what to do. She does not want to tell her parents because they are always singing her praises as being intelligent and prudent with money and if they knew the truth, they would be so disappointed.

Jackie has applied for 14 jobs now and has only had two interviews. She dropped out of the marketing course because her company was paying for it but when she was made redundant, they stopped any further payments.

In tears, Jackie embraces Paul who comforts her. They hold hands and continue walking through the park. On reaching the lake, they sit down on the grass, watching the ducks paddle around and begin to share some jokes.

"I haven't laughed like this for ages" says Jackie.
"It's good to see you laugh. I love it when you laugh.
And when you smile. You are so beautiful."
"Do you really think so?"
"Of course. Everything about you is beautiful. I
really like you."

There is silence. They stare at each other. Paul leans
over to Jackie and kisses her slowly. She kisses back for
a moment, and then pulls away as if to say I can't do
this. She looks away. Paul raises his right hand, places
it gently under her chin, and slowly turns her head
back to face his. They stare into each others eyes for
a moment. Nothing is said. They kiss.

Jackie has never kissed anyone like this before. She is
a virgin living in her preacher father's home. She has
never been in a relationship. She is feeling warmth
and a sensation that she has never felt before. It feels
wonderful. Her heart rate begins to increase. Her
eyes are closed. Her body is weak. Wrapped in the
arms of someone who cares for her. There is a
forbidden fruit feeling that appears in the back of her
mind. But the moment, the feeling, the emotion, just
feels wonderful. Just what she needs right now.

Jackie and Paul lie with their backs on the ground,
holding hands and looking up at the stars. What does
this mean? Paul is not saved. He is white. She is
black. The future seems uncertain. But the present
feels right.

Chapter 2

The offering has just been taken and Minister Campbell, the Assistant Pastor, has taken to the podium to bring the Sunday morning sermon. He is a tall, slim man, well dressed, looking polished and well groomed, thanks to Mrs Campbell. The other Ministers, including Pastor Ellington, are on the platform.

Minister Campbell is a firebrand. He is known as a dynamic speaker who tells it like it is. Outside of the church platform he is a mild mannered young man of 36, who is married without children. An office manager by profession, and fully dedicated to the service of God.

He preaches several times a month and is able to hold the attention of the congregation on every occasion because of the simplicity of his message and how he delivers it. For some time now, many people in the church have complained that the same people are preaching all the time and that other people do not get the chance. This has not affected Minister Campbell. He preaches with conviction every time he is called to give the sermon for the day.

"The second coming of Christ is not a myth" he declares passionately. "Jesus said that He has gone to prepare for us a place, that where He is, there may we be also. He told his disciples that He must go away so that the Comforter, who the Father would send in His name, would come. Even though we may have heard this preaching for years, since we were children, that Jesus is coming back again, and He still has not come yet, let us take more heed because His appearance is now nearer than when we first believed. Let us therefore take the more earnest heed to the things that we have heard, lest at any time we should let them slip.

In Acts chapter one when we read the account of the ascension, when Jesus was taken up in the air, and a cloud removed Him from sight, the angels that appeared told the believers who were standing there gazing up into the sky, that this same Jesus whom they had seen taken up into heaven, would come again in like manner. So heaven confirmed the message that Jesus is coming back. All over the pages of the New Testament we read about the Lord's return.

This is part of the Gospel message. That Jesus died for our sins, and that He was resurrected, that He ascended into heaven to be seated on the right hand of god, and that He is coming back. The story is true. Therefore, if we believe that the message is true, what are we doing about it? How are we preparing to meet the Lord when He comes? Will He find us faithfully serving Him, or will He find us doing our own thing?

Will He find us with oil in our vessels like the five wise virgins, or will He find us with sin in our lives and so He will say to us, depart from me I know you not.

Look around brethren. The day of the Lord draweth near. No man knows the day nor the hour when He will put in his appearance, but we can see the signs of the times and we are confident that we are living in the last days. So live christian live. Live a life of holiness. If you cannot preach a word live. Every man must work out his own salvation, and every man will answer for the things that he has done."

After preaching for nearly an hour, Minister Campbell gave an altar call. He called those who do not know the Lord Jesus as their personal Saviour to come for prayer and to receive the Lord in their lives. Many people came forward. He also called for those in the congregation who know that their lives are not right and they need to repent and cover themselves under the blood. Altar workers were kept busy in prayer and the laying on of hands, as over 50 people came forth for prayer.

Such services at Mount Zion Refuge are not uncommon. The people genuinely love the Lord and when they hear the word of god being preached, they humble themselves and fall in line with it. Some people come repeatedly to the altar because they have not yet learned how to sanctify themselves throughout the week and therefore do not know how to live an overcoming life. Spiritually, they are up one day and down the next, but they are sincerely trying, and each time they fall, they rise up again, repent, and go on serving the Lord. Over time, they will learn to become more stable and mature in Christ and overcome these personal weaknesses.

Later that week, Jackie got a phone call to say that she was successful in her latest job interview and the company would like to offer her the position as a Marketing Officer. A delighted Jackie accepted, and called her parents to tell them the good news. Dad was out, at the church vestry, preparing some teaching notes for Sunday, but mum was home and was delighted to hear the news.

Paul, on hearing the news, was also pleased for her and he asked her to meet him after work so that he could take her out to celebrate. She met him at his workplace at 5pm and the two went shopping in the city centre. He bought her some clothes to wear to her new job and they went to a Japanese restaurant afterwards.

On the way home she realised that she could not go home with all those clothes because her parents would ask where she had got the money from to buy them. She didn't want to be placed in a position of having to lie to them, so she asked Paul if he could keep them at his house until her first pay day.

Although the relationship had been going on for a few weeks, Jackie did not want Paul to come anywhere near the church or to be known to her parents. She was sure that they would not approve and that the church would not understand. In her mind, as a christian woman, she was just friendly with someone, and even though she now had feelings for him, she knew that she should not be in such a relationship, but knowing this psychologically and doing something about it are two different things. Paul makes her laugh. He is there for her emotionally. He respects her. She can talk to him. Confide in him. Share personal things with him. She was not willing to let this go, at least, not yet.

On reaching Paul's home, they went inside. It is a well furnished two bedroom house not far from Manchester City's football stadium.

"Where is your mother?" Jackie asks.
"She is in Sheffield, visiting her elder sister in hospital. She'll be back tomorrow. Come let me show you around." Paul proceeds to take her on a tour of the house. It's over quite quickly as men generally do not take long to show people around their homes. They do it in a matter of fact way, saying things like "this is the bedroom. And over here is the bathroom" without going to the detail that a woman would.

"This is a nice place" declares Jackie.
"Thanks. My mum does all the creative stuff. I just provide the money. It's a good deal really."

Having finished showing her around, they finally sit in

the lounge. "I would like you to meet my mother" he says. "Yes, sure thing" she replies. "It would be nice to see what she looks like."

Paul puts on some soft music. He turns the lights down a bit and snuggles up to Jackie on the sofa. The two talk for a while and share a joke or two. Paul has always had the ability to make her laugh, which is one of the qualities that she likes about him.

Jackie is beginning to feel a bit vulnerable and that she should not be there, not alone with a man in his house, especially a man that she likes. It is simply unnecessary temptation. She wants to leave, but at the same time she doesn't want to. Paul is stroking her hair and talking to her. He tells her how much she means to him. That he thinks about her all the time and that he has never met anyone quite like her.

Jackie kisses him. To the music of Nat King Cole, Paul puts his right hand behind her back and enjoys the kiss. After a few minutes, he moves his hand up her blouse and rubs her soft back gently as he continues to kiss her. Her ebony flesh feels smooth and warm to the touch.

Jackie's heartbeat starts to run wild. She is panting for breath. Her eyes are closed. Paul brings his right arm around from her back, across her side, and to her chest, gently caressing her breasts as he holds her.

Jackie's body is tingling with emotion and sexual

desire. A feeling that she has never experienced before. She is wet inside her knickers. Scared, but excited. Emotional, yet calm.

"Get out of the house now" a voice inside her head is saying, "Leave this place."
She is confused. "Fornication is sin" the voice says. "You will go to hell."

Jackie opens her eyes and pulls away from Paul. Her body is saying "yes" whilst her head is saying "no." She knows that what she is about to do is wrong, but she wants it. The feeling is overwhelming. She cannot help it. She doesn't want to stop.

"It's alright baby" says Paul, as he sees the hesitation in her eyes.
"I have never done anything like this before. I am a virgin."
"That's OK. I know what I am doing. I will be gentle. I won't hurt you. You are so beautiful. I just want to share this moment with you and get closer to you."

He begins to kiss and fondle her again. This time she does not resist and the two make love right there on the sofa. Paul does not rush. He takes his time and leads her gently. Their clothes are spread all over the floor. Sounds of ecstasy and groans are heard. On reaching orgasm, Jackie cries out and grabs Paul tightly, pulling him down on top of her naked body, trembling all over. She hugs him. With both bodies panting and sweating, they remain in that position for some time, basking in post-sexual satisfaction.

"That was wonderful" she says, "I never dreampt that it was like this."

At the Pastor's house

Pastor and Mother Ellington are wondering what has happened to Jackie. It's now 10.30 pm and there has been no word from her. Neither Dawn nor David had seen or heard from their sister and it was unusual for her to be out so late without a phone call.

At that moment, Jackie comes into the house "Hi mum, hi dad" she says and runs upstairs to the bathroom. Her mother follows her.

"Are you alright?" she calls from outside the door.
"Yes I am fine" Jackie answers. "I am just fixing myself a bath"
"We were getting a little worried as we had not heard from you."
"Sorry I didn't phone mum. I was out celebrating getting my new job."
"OK darling. I'll see you in the morning. Your father and I were waiting to go to bed."
"Ok mum. Say goodnight to dad for me."

Jackie begins to wash away her sexual smells so that there wouldn't be any give away signs.

During service on Sunday morning, Jackie begins to

feel condemned. She feels ashamed of what she has done. There is no-one that she feels she can talk to about the matter and so she just cries on her knees at the altar. Elder Samuels prays for her, asking the Lord to meet her needs and to grant her the desires of her heart.

She sobs and decides to end the relationship with Paul. After service she calls him to break the news. He refuses to accept it and says that he loves her. She says that she loves him too but that it is over because it is wrong.

"When you are with me does it feel wrong?" he asks.
"Well, no, but I can't. I am a christian. My father is the Pastor. I just can't do this."
"But he preaches about love doesn't he. So what is wrong with you loving me?"
"It's because you are not saved"
"But you love me anyway. And whenever I meet a christian, they say "Jesus loves you", so if you love me and Jesus loves me, what is the problem?"

"You don't understand" says Jackie and begins to cry.
"I won't let you go" says Paul. "I will come to your church on Sunday to see you if I have to."
"No you can't do that" she says, quite alarmed.
"Well I will if I have no choice."

A voice is heard from downstairs calling Jackie's name. It's her mother calling her to dinner with the family.
"I have to go now" she tells Paul. "We'll talk soon"

"No wait" he says, but the line goes dead. Quickly Jackie dries her eyes, tries desperately to control her emotions, and proceeds downstairs.

That evening, Jackie was even more sure that she has to break off the relationship with Paul. It's getting too risky. She has too much to lose. She has already lost her virginity and this she will never get back. Once gone, it is gone forever. And the memory of her fornication and the regret it brings, will last forever.

But at the back of her mind is the pain of losing Paul. She knows that she loves him but the situation is really loving on the edge.

The next day, Paul meets her after work and the two begin to talk. All the while Jackie explains why she, as a good christian woman cannot be with an unsaved man, and all the while she herself does not want to accept it. She is speaking from her principles and her faith position, but not out of conviction. Her feelings for Paul are very strong and she knows what she feels in her heart. She decides to keep seeing him.

Over the next couple of weeks, Paul and Jackie are spending more and more time with each other. Every now and then, they would be seen together by someone in the church. Pretty soon, word begins to spread that she is seeing someone. Some people who hear the news refuse to listen to such gossip, but others are intrigued. Could it be true? The pastor's daughter?

After prayer meeting one Tuesday night, an elder sister in the church took Mother Ellington aside and informs her of the gossip that is going around about Jackie. Mother Ellington is outraged. "How could these people think such a thing about my daughter? She is saved and we didn't bring her up like that."

That night, back at the Ellington house, she tells Pastor about the rumour. He becomes angry and starts talking about carnal people who should get a grip on themselves and who should know better. He is determined to get to the heart of the matter and to find out who these culprits are. Such talk is undermining his credibility as Pastor he feels. His house must set an example and be a model. What will the people think of his ministry if he cannot control his own house he says to himself.

For years, there has been a sign in his lounge that says "As for me and my house, we will serve the Lord" and he is very proud of that saying and is determined to live up to it, so help him God. Any challenge to it by gossipers will not be tolerated.

The following day he calls Jackie. She leaves her room where she was sharing a joke with her sister Dawn and comes down stairs. "Yes dad" she says to a stern faced father.

He tells her about the rumours that have been spreading about her carrying on with someone outside the church. "Some people say that they have seen you together on the bus, some window shopping, and someone has seen you holding hands with this person. Is this true?"

Jackie denies this and asks who has been saying such things. Her father says that he does not know who is involved or how it started but that the devil is a liar and that he will get to the bottom of it. "I am not going to stand for any such nonsense" he says.

Chapter 3

Pastor Ellington spent much of the week trying to find out the source of the rumours concerning his daughter. He had to be careful because in asking some people about it, he would be giving them information that they did not otherwise know, and he would, in effect, be spreading the rumours himself. Others said that they had heard the rumour but didn't know where it had started from. This left Pastor none the wiser and the trail went cold.

He was determined to bring it into the open with a pastoral rebuke on Sunday morning. If he could not name and shame the persons responsible, which he would have done in private, he was now set on shaming, if not naming the persons responsible in public.

It is 11.30 am and Elder Samuels is teaching in the Sunday School. A Barbadian by birth, he has been with the church since its inception and has served faithfully in his office since his appointment some nine years previous. Many felt, as he does, that he should have been made the Assistant Pastor when the vacancy occurred, but Pastor Ellington chose Minister

Campbell instead. Although Elder Samuels initially resented being passed over in favour of the younger man, and feels that being a Barbadian probably had something to do with it, he now feels that Minister Campbell has shown enough dedication and seriousness about the role to qualify him for the office and he fully respects his ministry.

Today, Elder Samuels is continuing his three part series on the resurrection of Jesus Christ. In the first part, he took the saints through the authenticity of the Bible record and proved from many sources that it can be totally relied upon as authentic, and that the word of god is true. His point was that if we can all agree that the Bible is the word of god and that all scripture was given by the inspiration of god and is therefore profitable for doctrine and instruction, then we should not have any trouble believing that Jesus rose from the dead because it is written all over the New Testament and spoken of in the Old Testament.

In part two, he outlined chronologically what took place from the moment when Jesus cried aloud "It is finished" on the cross and died, to the three days that He spent under the earth, His resurrection as described by the Gospel writers, through to His ascension back to heaven 40 days later, and finally the promise of His return.

Today, in the final part of the three part series, Elder Samuels is going through historical sources that are outside the Bible that confirms that Jesus was resurrected. His intent is to empower the believers to be able to answer any skeptic or critic about the truth of the resurrection. To reinforce his teaching, he calls out two brothers to sit on chairs at the front of the congregation and asks them to do some role play. He asks one person to be a skeptic and the other person to be himself and answer the points that are made against the resurrection.

Brother Henry, acting as the skeptic would make comments such as "I would like to believe the Bible but I can't believe some of the myths that are in it such as Jesus' resurrection. We all know that when someone is dead, he is dead, and so as an intelligent person, I can't take Christianity too seriously"

In front of everyone, Brother Sammy, being himself, had to answer Brother Henry and debate with him the issue. "But man wrote the Bible" says the skeptic, "and even the Bible itself says that we should not put our trust in man because the arm of the flesh will fail. So why should we believe the people who wrote the Bible."

The debate went on for a few minutes until Brother Sammy got stuck and could not answer any more questions. Elder Samuels thanked them both and called two other people and they went through the same role play but dealt with other aspects of the debate surrounding the resurrection.

When this was concluded, Elder Samuels said that he had conducted this role play exercise to see how much the brethren took in when he was teaching, for if they had not grasped his teaching, then they would not be in a position to answer the points made by the skeptic.

"We believe in the resurrection" he told the congregation, "but some people do not, and we have to be able to discuss it with them and show that the Bible record is true. We must have an answer to what they say and therefore we must study the scriptures for ourselves. Many Christians do not do their own Bible study, they merely read a psalm or a chapter here and there when they have a few minutes to spare or before going to work. But we have to study to show ourselves approved unto God. If we don't study the Word, then we will not be able to rightly divide the word of truth and we will not be able to contend earnestly for the faith."

The children begin to come into the main hall from their Sunday School classes and so Elder Samuels wraps up his teaching and hands over the service to Evangelist Morrison. "Blessed be the name of the Lord" is her chosen song and the church joins in for a time of worship. The four musicians are at their posts playing skilfully. With smiling faces everywhere in a joyful atmosphere, the people sing with conviction. A group of sisters begin to dance in the spirit. Many are clapping. Their bodies swaying to the beat of the music.

After a few lively choruses, Evangelist Morrison says that they should go deeper into worship and she begins to sing a few slower, consecrated songs. Songs such as:

The Lord is blessing me, right now (2 times)
He woke me up this morning, started me on my way
The Lord is blessing me right now, right now, right now.

And

Lord Jesus, we enthrone you, we proclaim you our King
Standing here in the midst of us, we raise you up with
our praise
And as we worship build your throne (3 times)
Come Lord Jesus and take your place.

The presence of the Lord comes down in the meeting and the saints get lost in worship. Sister Mary and a few other women are slain on the floor and are being covered up by several sisters because their skirts are fairly short and much of their legs are being exposed. A number of men are pretending not to look whilst others turn their heads in the other direction and continued to worship.

Some are speaking in tongues. Mother Ellington is at the altar laying hands on two sisters and praying for them. As the service continues, some of the saints testify, two brothers exhort, the choir sings "Amazing Grace" and the offering is taken. It was now 1.30 pm and Pastor Ellington rises to preach.

Before he gets into his message he said that there was

a rather disturbing matter that he wanted to clear up before he gave his sermon. He told the church that some people, busy-bodies as he called them, were spreading a malicious rumour about one of his daughters, and that it was a lie and they must stop. "I don't know who this person, or who these people are" he declared, "but I am giving them an open rebuke this morning and demanding that they stop peddling these rumours. It is not good for the church and it is certainly not good for my daughter."

With that, he began to preach his message. Some in the congregation began to wonder which daughter he was speaking about or what the rumours were. Some thought that it was Jackie because she is "into everything" whilst others thought that it must be Dawn as she is the quieter of the two and "still waters run deep."
Apart from who Pastor was talking about, there is the what. What is the nature of the rumour? What is being said? Is it a scandal? Or a big sin? Is it jealousy of some kind, or did the person get caught doing something that she should not have? With all this wondering by a portion of the congregation, the sermon being preached was not being given the attention it deserved. Whispers were going around and notes were being passed from one person to the other asking if they knew anything.

When the service ended, a number of people, trying to fish for information, approached Jackie and said that she must not worry about rumours but that she must be strong. They were trying to see if she would acknowledge that the rumours were about her or if she would say that they have nothing to do with her, in which case it would then have to be Dawn. They tried the same thing with Dawn but both sisters had spoken about it before the service and anticipated that some nosey people would be asking questions after the announcement by Pastor. They had therefore decided that they would both say that they never worry about rumours, leaving the enquirer none the wiser.

Back at home, Jackie is in her bedroom, lying on her back and looking up at the ceiling. She is thinking about her life and what has happened recently. Principally, she is thinking about Paul. She is uneasy about having a secret part of her life that is hidden from her family and from the church. This is a new experience for her. It is not how she had imagined things would turn out. She had always felt that she would meet a lovely christian brother and marry him in a big church wedding, with her father giving her away and her mother looking proud.

That is the christian way. That is her preferred way. But now, what can she do. She has mixed emotions. On the one hand, she is in love with an unsaved person and if that is not bad enough, this person is white, which complicates things. Her parents have never said anything against white people and certainly have never told any of their children not to get involved with other races, but somehow, the unspoken expectation was that they would marry within their race. That they would marry a black person.

In all of Jackie's fantasies and dreams, the person that she was with in her imaginations, was always black. She would never consciously seek after a white person, even though she does not consider herself to be prejudiced in any way. But what can she do? She has fallen for a white man. A man that loves her. A man who respects her, listens to her, takes care of her, and a man that makes her feel special, valued, and important.

There are quite a few sisters in the church who are in their 30's and 40's and are still waiting for a husband. Some say that it does not bother them and that they are married to Jesus, but do they really mean it and are they happy? Some admit that being single does bother them and that they would really like to fall in love and get married.

Love is hard to find Jackie tells herself, and it can come in the most unexpected of places. She cannot, will not, deny the love that she feels for Paul, even though she fully understands the consequences of her actions and the problems that it will cause. Maybe Paul will get saved, she thinks. When she talks to him about church, he does listen. In fact, he has wanted to visit Jackie's church for a while but she has held him back for fear of what people might say.

A few days later, Paul and Jackie are on the 192 bus

heading for Paul's home. Jackie has agreed to go and meet Paul's mother, something he has wanted her to do for a long time. In preparation, Mrs Claire McKenzie is busy in her kitchen preparing the dinner. A slightly built woman wearing a black dress and glasses, she has already vacuumed the house, polished the furniture and brought out her best cutlery for the occasion. Today is special she feels because it is rare for Paul to want to bring home any of his girlfriends.

She realises that Paul's relationships never last long and he just seems to have one fling after another, but nothing really serious. This time, he has been talking about a very special girl and he wants to bring her home to meet his mum. This must be serious says Mrs McKenzie to herself and she wants to make a good impression.

Since her bitter divorce when Paul was very young, she has not had another man in her life and so Paul has had no role model in the home to look up to. She tries her best but realises that she cannot do the job of a father. She just wants her son to be happy and to meet someone that he can finally settle down with.

At the front of the house, the happy couple arrive at the gate. Jackie is fussing about how she looks and is feeling a bit nervous. This is a new experience for her – meeting a possible future mother-in-law, and she does not know how to act. "Just be yourself" Paul says comfortingly, "she will love you the way I love you."

On entering the house, Paul greets his mother with a kiss and introduces Jackie. Mrs McKenzie pauses for a moment, her eyes getting wider, her mouth dropping. She composes herself quickly, smiles, and says "hello Jackie, it's so nice to meet you. Paul has told me so much about you."

Paul did not tell her previously that Jackie was a black. All the time that he was talking about that special someone, she took it for granted that the person he was speaking about was white, as all his girlfriends in the past had been.

Whilst on the outside, Mrs McKenzie said all the right things during the evening, and did her best to be pleasant, at the back of her mind she was telling herself that this relationship will be like all the others ie it won't last. I can see why Paul would be attracted to her she says to herself, because Jackie is a very pretty girl. She has a good figure and she is a very nice person, of obvious good character and upbringing. But a mate for Paul? No chance. "And me having half cast grand kids? I don't think so."

Jackie enjoyed meeting Mrs McKenzie and found her to be a very good host. Paul was pleased that the two women in his life were getting on so well. He was sitting in the armchair watching his mother show Jackie the family albums and they were both laughing at some embarrassing pictures of him when he was young, when he was sitting on a potty and eating a biscuit, and another when he had lost all his front teeth.

There were hardly any photos of Paul's father and Mrs McKenzie explained that she threw most of them away, but kept back a few so that Paul would see what his father looked like when he grew up.

The evening ended a success, with Mrs McKenzie hugging Jackie and telling her to come back soon. Paul walked her to the bus stop and waited with her until the bus arrived. Everything had turned out well they thought and were both happy. Maybe it will work out after all Jackie thought to herself as she kissed Paul goodnight and hopped on the bus heading for home.

Chapter 4

A meeting is taking place in Pastor Ellington's home. The senior ministers of the church are meeting in his private study to discuss what they feel is the deterioration of standards in the church. Some of the women in the church, in particular the younger women, are dressing a bit too loosely and this has given rise to some complaints by the older mothers.

Present in the meeting are Pastor Ellington, Minister John Campbell, the Assistant Pastor, Elder Samuels, Evangelist Beverley Morrison, the only female member of the senior team, and Deacon Hudson.

They are all convinced that the presence of the Lord is real in their meetings and that the teaching and preaching is good. They have not been watering down the Gospel to attract the crowd but have been preaching the truth. However, they are concerned now at the standard of dressing by some believers, and having seen but not dealt with the situation sooner, they now have a more serious problem, as more and more sisters are dressing loosely. In the face of complaints, they are now forced to act and this meeting has been called to decide what to do about it.

"Sanctification must be seen outwardly if it is present inwardly" declares Minister Campbell, the Assistant Pastor. "What are these sisters saying when they dress so inappropriately in church. What messages are they giving out to the men?"

"But sanctification is much more than how we dress" states Evangelist Beverley Morrison. "In fact, it's only a tiny part of what sanctification is all about. And why are we only talking about the sisters? What about the brothers?"

"If brothers are dressing inappropriately, we will talk to them also" replied Minister Campbell, "we don't exclude anyone. It's just that the sisters are more visibly carnal in their dress sense"
"That's a bit strong" Evangelist Morrison replies.
"Well it's true, and if we don't deal with it, then the church will go down."
"And if it goes down, the women are to blame, is that what you are saying?"
"No that's not what I am saying"
"Well make yourself clear, what are you saying?"

At this point Pastor Ellington steps in and says that everyone must calm down because they are all on the same side, the side of righteousness. He says that he has noticed that some sisters are wearing skirts that are too short in church. "It is alright when they are standing up but when they sit down and cross their legs, they are showing a bit too much. From being on the platform, I can see thighs and I have even seen knickers a few times."

"That's true" interrupted Elder Samuels, "and some of their tops look fine but when they lean over to pick something up, we can sometimes get a good view of their assets. And when they are slain in the spirit and are rolling over on the ground, we can often see up their skirts."

"Well you should not be looking" comments Evangelist Morrison looking sternly at Elder Samuels. "You can't help it sometimes" he replies, "its right there in your face. I like to see a nice pair of breasts like any man, but in the privacy of my own home, with my wife, not in church when we come before the Lord. That's unacceptable."

After much discussion, the meeting came to the consensus that Pastor Ellington would use his pastoral authority to say to the church that skirts should be worn well below the knee and that this would be now the dress code for sisters in the church.

They then began to speak about women wearing trousers in the church. "We need a line on that also" declared Deacon Hudson. "Women should not wear trousers at all because it is unbiblical. Their sexy curves cause a distraction in the church."

"There is nothing wrong with trousers" Evangelist Morrison points out. "I admit, some sisters wear really tight or figure hugging ones but you can't ban the wearing of trousers because of them."

"Figure hugging trousers are too sexy to be worn in church sister" Deacon Hudson responds.

"Do you find them sexy Deacon?"

"No ... not me ... well, yes I do, but I am able to blank it out of my mind and continue to think spiritual thoughts. The problem is that some brothers might not be able to and there is also the unsaved men in our midst also. We must think about them."

"If a woman wears trousers that are not figure hugging, some brothers will still find it sexy" said Evangelist Morrison. "If they wear long dresses, some men will still find them attractive. Whatever we sisters do, men being men, will still have all sorts of imaginations going on in their minds and so their flesh is the problem, not the trousers."

The debate started to get a bit heated with Evangelist Morison defending the rights of women. "If it's not our hair, it's our make-up. If it's not make-up, then its trousers. We women are always picked on under the banner of sanctification, and the brothers just get away scott free. No-one ever says anything about them."

Unable to agree, the meeting broke up without a decision being taken on the wearing of trousers. They agreed to revisit the subject at a later date, but for now, Pastor would only speak about wearing longer skirts and to advise the sisters to be careful of their tops.

The following evening, Mother Ellington, went to Jackie's bedroom to speak with her. She asked how her new job was going and if everything was alright. Jackie assured her that everything was fine. Her new boss was very nice and she is enjoying the work.

"Is there anything that you would like to tell me?" she asks her daughter.
"No, not really mum. What do you mean?"
"Well it's just that you seem to be acting a bit differently these days. Your coming home pattern has changed. You come in later than you used to and you don't call to say where you are as much as you used to."

"Sorry about that mum. I shall try and be a bit more considerate."

"You have also been coming home every now and then and going straight to the bathroom without saying hello to me and dad first."

"Sometimes I am just bursting to go to the toilet. I drink a lot of water during the day."

"No dear, this is not to take a pee. You run the bath. And I have been wondering, why would a young woman not interact with her family first, maybe have dinner, and then run a bath if she wanted one. What I wonder could be the reason."

Jackie begins to feel nervous. She says nothing.

"As your mother, I have certain instincts and I know when you are hiding something. You have never been a child that could lie very well. I know something is up Jackie. Now what is it?"

Jackie remains silent, not knowing what to say. She wants to tell her mother but she is afraid.

"Jackie, I know that you are seeing someone. Isn't that right?"

Jackie sighs, takes a deep breath, and nods her head.

"I have noticed how you have been acting lately and I can see the look in your eyes. It is the look of someone in love. And I know that you have been sexually active also. Isn't that true?"

"How do you know that?"

"I am a woman darling and I can see the signs. It's true isn't it?"

"Yes mum."

For the next hour, mother and daughter spoke about the situation. Jackie tells her about Paul, how they met and how the relationship started and developed. She tells her that she did not go looking for a man but that he just came in her heart one day and has found a deep place there. "I am in love mummy for the first time in my life" she says as some tears run down her cheeks.

Mother Ellington remembers what it was like for her when she first fell in love and how overwhelming a feeling it was. She remembers how her heart was broken when her boyfriend went off with another woman and how she was distraught and had to cope with life afterwards.

"I can't tell you to stop seeing this man because you are an adult now and you can make your own choices. But darling sex before marriage is not right in the sight of god. You know that we preach against that in Mount Zion Refuge. What church does this Paul go to?"

"He doesn't go to church mum. He is not a christian."
"Oh Jackie, Jackie, that's even worse. My god, what are we going to do?"

Jackie continues to cry. Her mother holds her in a warm embrace. This is her eldest daughter going off the rails. Her firstborn child left home early and is backslidden and has a child out of wedlock. Now her second child is committing fornication with a sinner. "My god, what are we going to do? What are we going to do?"

Chapter 5

Pastor Ellington is in the home of Brother and Sister Griffiths. They have been married for 18 months now and are having some marital problems. Brother Griffiths is in a good job but he hides a lot of money from his wife for fear that she will spend it on unnecessary things. He keeps a tight reign on the purse strings in the home and limits how much his wife can spend in any one month.

Although working herself, and earning a decent salary, Sister Griffiths is resentful towards her husband and this has manifested itself in many different ways. She is often distant, emotionally unattached, and when it comes to the bedroom department, she frequently gets an headache. The couple are drifting apart and they have lost the flame of romance. They still love each other but they are stuck in a rut and do not know how to reignite the flame.

Pastor is counselling them on honesty and trust in a relationship and tells them that they must reach an agreement over finances which they are both happy with. If either side is unhappy, then the plan will not work he tells them.

He also tells brother Griffiths that if he continues to stifle his wife and not enable her to develop her nest, then he will have one miserable woman on his hands and it will be his fault. Let her be free to make spending decisions around the home because it is to build up her home and not to pull it down.

When Pastor leaves and returns home, he finds his wife sitting alone in the dining room. He enters and greets her with a kiss on her forehead. "Is everything alright darling?" he asks, as he sees her looking a bit troubled.

"Please sit down" she says, "I have something to tell you."

For the next twenty minutes they talk about Jackie's situation. Pastor Ellington is surprised and angry. How could his daughter lie to him in this way? How could she carry on with an unsaved man? Had she learnt nothing from his preaching over the years? And the church, he publicly rebuked those people who were saying that Jackie was seeing someone, and now he finds out that those rumours were true all along.

He storms out of the dining room saying "where is she" and Mother Ellington follows him calling him back. "Don't do anything stupid Joseph" she says trying to keep up with him. Jackie is in her pyjamas in the lounge, having a cup of tea and watching the 10 o'clock news on TV. Dawn is sitting beside her texting a friend and David is on the internet in the corner of the room.

Pastor comes into the lounge and breaks the tranquillity. He tells Dawn and David to leave the room and begins to confront Jackie about Paul. He shouts at her and tells her that she is a sinner. He says that he will not tolerate this type of behaviour in his house and that she must break off the relationship immediately.

A stunned Jackie tries to reason with him but he refuses to listen. "He is not saved, so any relationship with him is out of the question. The Bible says "Be ye not unequally yoked together with unbelievers, for what fellowship has righteousness with unrighteousness, and what communion has light with darkness." You must end this relationship and repent now!"

"But dad, I love him" says Jackie
"You can't love him. He is not a christian. You only think that you love him. I forbid you to see him."

The two of them go head to head, father angrily and forcefully, and daughter quietly and tearfully. Mother Ellington is keeping out of it, for now. She is watching but not intervening, consciously allowing her husband, the head of the home, to deal with the situation.

"How will this make me look in the eyes of the church?" says Pastor. "I will look a fool. I will be a laughing stock."

Later on in the conversation, when Jackie continues to refuse to stop seeing Paul, she let it slip that he is white. Her father looked horrified. "What!" he says, "a white man!" For him, this bad situation had just become worse. He shouted some more at Jackie and told her that she had one week to break it off or else. She ran out of the room sobbing. Pastor sat in an armchair wondering how this could happen. Mother Ellington moved closer to sit next to him. She held his hand and didn't say a word.

For the rest of the week, Jackie did her best to stay out of the reach of her father. When at home, she spent most of the time in her bedroom. Dawn and David came in to cheer her up and to offer support. Occasionally, Mother Ellington would come in to check that she was alright or bring her a snack.

At the end of the week, Pastor Ellington called Jackie and asked her if she had broken off the relationship yet as the deadline was up. Jackie said no and tried to reason with her father. He shouted at her some more and when she could not get a word in, she raised her voice and said "I am pregnant!"

With that, there was silence in the room. You could hear a pin drop. Pastor stormed out. Mother Ellington came over to Jackie and asked her if she was sure. She was. Two tests had proved it.

Ten minutes later, Pastor came back in the room and announced that Jackie was no longer in the Choir and that she must not help with the Sunday School. Furthermore, she has to pack her bags and leave home. "I cannot have a child of mine, under my roof, so blatantly disobeying me and carrying on in this way. You spread your bed, you lie in it."

A shocked Jackie appealed to her mother but mother says that she cannot go against her husband and the pastor of the church. Jackie runs to her room in tears. When she is able to speak, she calls Paul and tells him what has happened. He consoles her and says that she can move in with him until she finds a place.

The next day, Mother Ellington returns home from work and finds a note from Jackie saying that she is sorry to disappoint them but she is in love and won't give up Paul. Her clothes are missing and there is no indication as to where she has gone. Pastor returns home and hears the news. He feels no remorse and says that she has brought this on herself. David and Dawn are in a state of shock and want to know where their big sister is.

For days there is no contact. They tried calling Jackie at work but her manager said that Jackie had asked for time off suddenly and that he had given her leave. Jackie's mobile was left in her bedroom, presumably by accident, so there was no way of reaching her. Everyone hoped that she would show up at church on Sunday morning.

Meanwhile, back at Paul's house, Jackie was making herself comfortable. His mother did not know about Jackie's pregnancy or that her father had asked her to leave home. She was finishing off a late shift at her cleaning job and Jackie had moved into her home during the day.

On arriving home at 8.30 pm, she met Paul at the door who greeted her and said that he had something to ask her. On seeing Jackie, she began wondering what this could all be about. Paul apologised that he was not able to speak with her first, but he had tried ringing her workplace but she was not there. She had in fact been working an extra shift on another site, and she does not have a mobile phone.

On hearing what had happened to Jackie, Mrs McKenzie was very sympathetic, but on hearing that Paul was asking her if Jackie could stay with them until she found a place of her own, she was less so. She agreed however, mainly because she felt that she had no choice. After all, it would look very bad if she said no, get out of my house.

Sunday morning at church

An anxious Mother Ellington kept thinking about Jackie and every time the door opened, she turned round to see if it was her daughter coming in. Jackie's seat on the choir was empty. People were asking if she was unwell and were not getting a suitable answer.

Mother Ellington was asked to come with an exhortation but she declined and said that she is not ready and that preference should be given to the younger ministers to speak. Her heart was heavy. She was feeling a mother's pain. Pastor Ellington on the other hand, was unmoved and felt that Jackie had let herself down, and what had happened to her was purely down to the choices that she had made.

During the evening service, when it was clear that Jackie was not coming, and following more rumours being spread, Pastor stood up to make an announcement. He told the church that Jackie had strayed away from the faith and that she was in a relationship with an unsaved man. When she refused to end the relationship, he removed her from all positions in the church that she occupied and also asked her to leave home. Her place will be filled on the choir and someone will be found to teach her Sunday School class he told the brethren. He ended by asking the church to pray for her in the hope that she will come to her senses like the prodigal son, and return home in repentance.

What Pastor did not announce was the fact that Jackie was also pregnant, but word son got out and it spread all over the church. The pastor's daughter, going astray, and getting pregnant by an unsaved man, was big news.

Some people began criticising Pastor for taking her side originally and publicly chastising some saints for spreading rumours about Jackie. Others said that he was not to know because she was covering it up. One or two said that he should have known because he is supposed to be a spiritual man.

Many people were kind to Jackie saying that she is a good person and that she should not be condemned because she has made one mistake. They say that the Pastor acted too hastily in throwing her out of the house and that he should have been more considerate. After all, he preaches about love and forgiveness, so why couldn't he show some of that towards his own child.

A portion of the congregation felt that Jackie had brought shame on the church and that it was right that she should have been removed from the choir and asked to leave the Pastor's house.

Sister Marjorie and Sister Morgan were in conversation about the issue. Both were in their mid-fifties and both have been married for many years. They were intolerant of Jackie's behaviour and spoke harshly about "these young people" and the weakness of the flesh.

"Having sex is so overrated" says Sister Marjorie, who had not made love to her husband for eight months. "These young people should be putting away the lusts of the flesh and they shouldn't be caught up in this type of mess. They should learn how to fast and pray and stop looking man."

"That's right Sister, I stopped having sex with my husband 4 years ago because my body is the temple of the Holy Ghost and I want to keep it pure and I won't pollute it with fleshly things."

The truth is that the sexual experiences of these two women were not pleasant ones and there is not much passion and love in their marriages. They spent many frustrating nights looking up at the ceiling when their husband finished his business in a minute or two and hardly with any foreplay. During the days and weeks, they were busy doing their own thing and gave them no attention; then suddenly they would come into the bedroom at night and expect marital duties to be performed. There was no romance and no intimacy. The men would just get into bed, get down to business, then roll over and go to sleep. The women felt used, undervalued, and unloved.

Instead of working on their marriages and trying to rekindle the flame that was once there, they are both unsympathetic to any person caught up in any problem of Jackie's kind, and even when wedding announcements are made in church, they mutter to themselves saying that all they want is sex.

Among the Ministers, opinions were split between those who were backing the actions of the Pastor and those who were of the opinion that he was too harsh.

In all this Mother Ellington said nothing. She

publicly supported her husband as Pastor, but privately in her heart, she was sorrowful for her daughter and wanted her to return home. She too felt that he was too harsh and that he placed his own feelings of disappointment above the needs of his daughter. She saw how he spoke to her and how rough he was, and that it made the bad situation even worse.

In Paul's home

Four days after moving in, Jackie is sitting in the kitchen with Mrs McKenzie having a cup of tea. Paul is out at the gym with some guys from work.

"Would you like to know more about Paul?" his mother asks.
"Yes of course" replied Jackie.

Mrs McKenzie begins to tell Jackie about what Paul was like as a child and about his first love. How the girl broke his heart. She told of his many girlfriends over the years and said that Paul was not a man that could commit in a relationship. He moves from one girl to the next when he is bored with them. That has been his pattern over the years.

"Did you know that?"

"No, no I didn't" replied Jackie.

"He won't change. He is like his father. That is why

I had to divorce him. There is no future for you and Paul. Sorry to have to be the one to tell you this."

"Oh but you are wrong Mrs McKenzie, Paul and I love each other and we do have a future"

"No dear, you are just fooling yourself. Better quit now while you are ahead. It's more painful later on."
"Paul and I do have a future together. We love each other and I am expecting his child. We have talked about marriage."

A stunned Mrs McKenzie looks horrified. She was hoping to put off Jackie and subtly persuade her to call it off with her son, and now she hears that Jackie is pregnant. She is livid.

"No son of mine is going to marry a nigger!" she says. "I am not going to be the grandmother of mixed race children. No way!"

Jackie is shocked. And confused. Why is Mrs McKenzie now saying this, calling her a nigger, and talking like this, with such racism?

"I didn't know that you felt like this" she stated. "You have treated me well since I have been here and you have shown me kindness and care. Was that all a pretence?"

"I was willing to tolerate you for a while because I was convinced that Paul was only getting his oats and pretty soon he would grow tired of you and move on. Now I find out that the two of you are talking marriage and you are going to have his child. I can't have that. He is my only son and I'll be damned if he is going to marry a black girl. Over my dead body!"

"You can't stop us" declared Jackie.

"We'll see about that. I know my son better than you and you'll be history before you know it. I think that it's best for everyone if you had an abortion."

With that comment, Jackie gets up and goes to the bedroom. She refuses to argue with a racist in her own home. She begins to pack. Before she finishes, Paul arrives home. He sees his mother in a mood and asks if everything is alright. His mother tells him that the relationship with Jackie will not work and that he can do much better than her. Paul says no, that he loves her. His mother holds him by his hand and says "listen to me son, there are many more pretty girls out there, white girls, suitable girls."

Before she could finish her sentence, Paul pulls his hand away and says "where is Jackie?" He goes off to the bedroom and finds her crying. They talk for a few minutes and Jackie tells him what his mother had said to her. Paul is angry and goes back to confront his mother. The two argue a bit and Paul snaps at his mother and says that Jackie and the baby are his future whether she likes it or not. He storms into the bedroom and begins to pack himself. Jackie tells him no, but he refuses to listen and says that he cannot stay there any longer.

Mrs McKenzie pleads with Paul to stay but he leaves with Jackie and stops a passing taxi, asking the driver to take them to any nearby hotel. They check in for the night and in the morning they begin the hunt for a room. Two days later they find one and move out of the hotel. It's only a room in a house and they have to share the bathroom and kitchen with other tenants, but they are together. It seems that the world is against them, but they take comfort in each other and their love grows stronger.

Chapter 6

Three weeks has passed since Jackie left home. Her parents have not seen her in all that time and she has not visited the church. The family is getting worried. Mother Ellington is emotionally drained and cannot help crying inside for her daughter. She is wondering if she is alright. If she is eating? Where is she staying? Is she safe? David and Dawn are worried too and have asked around but no-one has seen Jackie. They have been to her work place but the manager told them that Jackie resigned suddenly and they don't have a forwarding address.

Pastor Ellington is outwardly hard, but inside he is being tormented. Joel, his eldest son, having heard that Jackie has left home, came round and had an argument with his father. He told him plainly what he thought of him as a parent and said that he has driven Jackie away just like he drove him away. He accused him of caring about the church more than he cared about his own children and that he was always busy with church issues and never had proper time with his children. Pastor told him to leave and he did so angrily.

Pastor Ellington is asking himself questions. Had he done the right thing? Could he have done anything different? What should he do now?

Meanwhile, the issue is causing a problem in the church. Some of the brethren side with Pastor and others are very critical of him. In the beginning, the majority of people sided with Pastor and felt that Jackie had brought the problem upon herself, but with news of her pregnancy, most people now believe that Pastor should do something to bring her back.

Every Sunday, Jackie's seat is empty on the choir and the situation is evident to all. It just won't go away. Pastor tried to fill the vacancy on the choir twice, but each time those he had asked said that they would like to join the choir but they do not feel that it is right to take Jackie's place.

The testimony services are not what they used to be either. Many people are not testifying like they used to, and the quality of the service is not the same. There is not the same reaction from the people when Pastor is preaching. An atmosphere seems to be hanging over the church. Mother Ellington has not said anything in church for many weeks now and people have guessed the reasons why.

Elder Samuels, after one mid-week service, spoke with Pastor and said that the church is divided over the Jackie issue and that he should call a Ministers meeting to discuss it. Pastor was reluctant, saying that it was a private family matter, but Elder Samuels insisted that it was also a church matter and that it was adversely affecting the church. He said that a few of the other Ministers agreed with him and that the meeting must be called soon. Reluctantly, Pastor agreed to the meeting.

Three days later, the meeting was held in the Vestry at the church. Present were the senior Ministers and the other ministers, a total of ten people. Pastor opened proceedings by saying that he had agreed to the meeting because there were some concerns amongst the Ministers about the situation with his daughter. He said that he felt that he had done the right thing as a father and as Pastor of Mount Zion Refuge, in keeping up the standards of the church. However he would now like to hear from the Ministerial team on the matter as it was they who wanted the meeting.

There was silence in the room. No-one wanted to speak first. "Well" said Pastor. "What are your views?" Everyone around the table, seated Board room style, looked slightly uneasy in their chair.

"Well Pastor" said Elder Samuels, "in speaking for myself, I would like to say that you had every right to do what you did with regards to Jackie because you are her father, but because the matter is causing a problem in the church, we feel that it needs to be sorted out. I have spoken to many people and I can tell you that everyone is troubled by the situation. Everyone loves Jackie and they also love you Pastor, but a sizeable group of people, especially the younger people, feel that you went overboard in throwing

Jackie out of the house. They say that you could have handled the situation with more compassion because we all make mistakes. They feel that you have written off your own daughter."

"That's nonsense" replied Pastor Ellington, "I have not written her off"

"I know that" continued Elder Samuels, "but this is what is being said."

"I have also spoken to many of the brethren" declared Evangelist Harrison, "and most are saying that you have upheld the integrity and standards of the church Pastor, but they would like to see Jackie restored to her position. They are worried for her soul and want her to return."

The meeting continued for two hours and at the end of it there was no conclusion. Pastor said that he had heard enough and thanked everyone for coming and making their views known, but that he has done what he has done for the good of the church and if anyone does not like it, then that's just unfortunate.

The next few church services were still being affected by the Jackie issue and everyone was talking about it. One sister got up during her testimony and started talking about Jackie, saying that the church should find her and bring her back. Pastor got up, took the microphone and stopped the sister. "Testimony time is for testimonies unto the Lord" he said "and this is not the place to start talking about Jackie."

The sister began to reply and said that everyone is concerned but Pastor cut her off and asked her to sit down. From that moment, no-one else stood up to testify. There was a lull in the meeting. Brother James who was leading the Testimony Service did not know what to do. He asked for more testimonies but no one stood up. He sang a song and afterwards there were still no testimonies so he handed the service back to the Ministers.

A few people walked out of the service shaking their heads. A few more followed. The Pastor stood to deliver his sermon, but try as he may he was distracted by the feeling in the atmosphere and the non-responsiveness of the people to his message. Normally, there would be a lot of "Amen"s and "hallelujahs" when he is preaching, but not this morning. The people politely listened but gave no reaction.

The message was cut short and the meeting finished early. The Ministers looked at each other and said that something had to be done. No-one knew what, but something had to be done.

That evening, the telephone rang in the Ellington household. It was Jackie. Everyone came around the phone to speak with her, so glad to hear her voice. Mother Ellington cried with the joy of hearing her daughter's voice and pleaded with her to come round to visit. Jackie said that she would soon visit but that she was ringing to inform everyone that she has set a date for her wedding.

Jackie gave them her new mobile number and asked her mother to tell dad. Mother Ellington again pleaded with her to come round and to bring Paul with her so that the family could meet him also. She agreed and said that they would come on Saturday.

When Saturday arrived, Paul and Jackie were making their way to the Ellington house feeling quite nervous. Jackie had not seen her father or the rest of the family since she moved out six weeks previous. What would be the reaction of her father?

On arrival, there were a lot of emotional hugs and kisses for Jackie and some pleasant handshakes for Paul. "Where is dad?" Jackie asked. "Oh, he is on his way home" said her mother.

Dawn and David quizzed their sister about what she had been doing, where she was staying etc. Mother Ellington did her best to make Paul feel at home and spoke with him about his work and interests. Suddenly, and with a rustle of keys at the door, Pastor came in. Jackie stood up and faced him nervously.

"Hello dad" she said. Her father walked over to her and hugged her without saying a word.
"This is Paul" she said and he stood up with his hand outstretched.

Pastor shook it and said "welcome to my home."

During the course of the evening, Pastor did not display any outward emotion. He was pleasant enough, and he asked a lot of questions. He could not believe that his daughter was still with this man when she should be coming to church and trusting the Lord for a good christian husband.

Mother Ellington was just happy that her daughter was safe and well, and back in her life.

"Dad, as mum told you, Paul and I are planning to get married on the 15th January. We want to get married before the child is born. Would you give me away?"

Pastor paused. He sighed heavily. "Sorry, but I cannot do that" he replied. There is a hush in the room. "I cannot give away my daughter to an unsaved man. I cannot do that. I want nothing to do with this wedding."

Jackie pleads with her father but he refuses to budge. She goes to her mother and asks her to talk to dad. "It's up to your father dear" she replies.
"It's nothing personal" Pastor says to Paul, "but as you are not a christian you would not understand. The Bible says that christians should not marry non-christians." With that, he gets up and walks out of the room.

Dawn says that dad will change his mind, but Jackie

knows that her father is as stubborn as she is when his mind is made up on a matter. Mother Ellington says that she will talk with Pastor and that she likes Paul. "I can see that you really love my daughter and I know that she loves you too. I admire such love and I wish you both a happy future together."

That meant so much to Jackie who embraced her mother and thanked her. Mother Ellington embraced Paul also and asked him to take good care of her daughter. He promised that he would.

On the way home, Jackie asks Paul about his mother. He tells her that he has been to see her twice and both times she refuses to attend the wedding. He is hoping that she will come round when she realises that he is serious and that the marriage will be going ahead.

Three weeks later, on the 14th October, Paul receives a phone call at work from the local hospital. His mother has just been brought in with a suspected heart attack. He rushes over to the hospital and she is by now on the operating table. He sits outside waiting to hear some news. Jackie arrives and hugs him. They both sit down and wait. And wait. Paul is especially worried because heart problems run in their family, and his aunt in Sheffield had a major scare a few months previous.

Eventually, a doctor comes out and tells them that Mrs McKenzie had died of heart failure and that they had tried all that they could do. Paul cries like a baby.

He has no father and now he has lost his mother. Being an only child was especially difficult. He felt that he had no-one besides Jackie.

The funeral takes place a week later and Paul reads the eulogy. There were not many people at the funeral. Jackie noticed that she was one of three black people there out of about sixty people. That did not matter to her. She was only thinking about Paul and how he was taking it all, and the truth was that he was taking it very badly. He breaks down at the laying of the body in the ground at the cemetery and Jackie has to hold him up. Paul has added sorrow because he did not get the chance to make it up with his mother. The last time they spoke, they were having an argument.

Sunday morning at Mount Zion Refuge

The congregation is smaller than usual. The truth is that about 350 believers have stopped coming to the church as they have lost confidence in the church leadership, in particular, in their Pastor. An anonymous letter written to the Pastor imploring him to restore Jackie fell on deaf ears. Having read the letter, he took offence to it and became more determined in his position. "What I have done, I have done" he says in a manner similar to Pilate when he was washing his hands at the trial of Jesus.

The young people in the church have been very vocal in saying that it is not fair what has happened to Jackie. Many of the older ones put the blame for it all

on Jackie, but a growing number is feeling sympathy for her situation, especially after hearing that she is pregnant. This is the charming young lady with the beautiful voice that sang in the Choir.
She taught many of their children in the Sunday School. She has had a clean record by any standards and this has been her only big mistake, at least that the church knows about. Surely such a person should not be cast aside for dogmatic reasons. Surely there must be compassion without accepting or condoning her sin.

That weekend, Jackie goes to visit the Ellington house. She wants to speak with her father again and to plead with him one more time to give her away. She tries and tries and eventually calls him stubborn. He gets angry and calls her a loose woman who has ran off with a white man and is living in sin. He says that she has brought shame to the family and that god will judge her for her sin of fornication.

Jackie runs out of his bedroom in a flood of tears and rushes downstairs. She trips and falls to the bottom in a heap, banging her head on the way down. She is in severe pain. Everyone rushes to her aid and an ambulance is called.

Mother Ellington goes with her into the ambulance and Pastor follows in a car with David and Dawn.

Half an hour later, Paul is seen rushing to the hospital in a taxi. On arrival, he runs straight in to Reception, finds out where Jackie is being kept, and runs off at speed in that direction. On finding the family outside the room crying, he fears the worst. "Is Jackie alright?" he asks. No-one answers.

He rushes into the room and a nurse stops him and tells him that he must wait outside because she is sedated and needs some rest. He explains who he is and she tells him that mother is fine, but she has lost the baby. Paul falls to his knees in deep distress.

Chapter 7

The following day, Sunday morning, Pastor Ellington is about to give his sermon. His message is about soul winning and evangelism. Mother Ellington is not in her usual seat on the platform next to him. She is furious at her husband for what has happened to Jackie and they had a blazing row the night before. She called him selfish and stubborn and said that he has driven half of his children away.

He argued that he has to set standards for the church even if it hurts but she replied that he is only thinking about himself and his image. She told him that his actions were based on selfish reasons as to what people might think about him as the Pastor with children going astray, and that he is not thinking about the needs of his children. Joel also had a serious argument with him at the hospital and said that he never wants to see him again.

Pastor Ellington carries on as normal. He is hurting terribly on the inside but feels that he has to put a brave face on because he is in church and he is the Pastor. He thinks of asking someone else to preach but feels that it might be taken as a sign of weakness.

He decides to press ahead.

After the offering is taken and the choir has sung their song, Pastor gets up, and walks to the podium.

"My message this morning is about soul winning and evangelism" he says, and he begins to outline the importance of witnessing to non-believers and winning souls for Christ. He says that it is the duty of every born again believer and that we all have a responsibility to do this and that it's not just a task for Ministers.

As he is speaking, a note is being passed around the church. The note says "Jackie lost her baby yesterday after an argument with Pastor." Stunned faces are to be seen all over the congregation. People begin to whisper. Pastor notices that something is wrong and that the people seem distracted.

Their body language is telling him that something is wrong, but he does not know what it is. He continues with his message, drawing reference to how Jesus spoke to the woman at the well of Samaria and pointing out that this was a classic example and blue print for effective soul winning.

He says that we can all speak to people on a one to one basis like how Jesus spoke to this woman, and that we don't all need to be Evangelists like Phillip who went to an entire city and won them over. In looking up from his notes, he notices some people leaving the service and shaking their heads. A murmur from across the congregation can be heard. The people seem restless. There is definitely something wrong, but what can Pastor do. He is in the middle of his sermon. He presses ahead, loses his train of thought a few times and tries desperately to get back on track. Preaching has never been so hard.

Finally, he finishes and sits down. Elder Samuels comes on and closes the service. Normally there is an altar call at the end of a preacher's message, but not today.

Later that day, Pastor receives a telephone call from Deacon Hudson informing him that a large proportion of the church is talking about leaving. He confesses that he too is thinking about leaving and that the church is at a cross roads. Pastor phones around to the other Ministers to see what they think, and after much discussion, it was agreed that a special members meeting would be called for Wednesday evening. An announcement to that effect was made that evening in the Sunday night service by Elder Samuels.

Mother Ellington did not attend the night service as she was too distraught and is still not talking with her husband, other than being polite. An urgent email was sent to all members on the church's database informing them of the special members meeting because, so many did not attend the Sunday night service. All over the world, in christian churches, it seems that Sunday morning services are well attended but a large number of people do not turn up for the night service.

Six miles away, in the Manchester Piccadilly area, Paul is making a cup of tea for Jackie in their rented room. She was released from hospital a few hours earlier and is still a bit weak. She is not saying much, mostly lying down and staring out of the window. Paul is trying to make her feel better but he too is emotionally distraught, and angry.

He is angry at the whole situation, of losing his child, and he blames Pastor Ellington. In fact, he now hates him with a passion. He wants to go round to his house and have it out with him. He would not do much talking with his mouth but he would do a lot of talking with his fists. But he knows that this would hurt his Jackie and that is the only reason why Pastor Ellington is not in the casualty department of the local hospital.

Paul has never been much of a church goer but he has been respectful of the Christian faith. He is now put off anything named church and he vows to never set foot in one again.

There is so much for him to think about. There is what to do with his mother's house. It has been left to him in her will, but does he want to live there? Does he want to sell it? At the moment none of that matters because his fiancé has just lost their baby.

Food is left on the table untouched. The television is watching itself. Paul lies next to Jackie. Both are in pain. Both crying inside. Both heavy with emotion.

At Mount Zion Refuge

It's Wednesday evening and about three and a half thousand people are present at the special members meeting. The atmosphere is intense. The Assistant Pastor, Minister Campbell, is chairing the meeting and is finding it awkward and personally very difficult. As the Assistant Pastor, he has been careful to be seen to display loyalty and has been motivated by the idea of going through tough times with his Pastor and not abandoning him. It was Pastor who appointed him and showed him favour when others felt that Elder Samuels should have been appointed in place of him.

Minister Campbell tries to be neutral in his views and tries to chair the meeting like he would do at work, and not reveal his hand. When forced to do so by a direct question, he finally says that he supports Pastor but says that if he was in the same situation, he would perhaps have dealt with it a little differently.

The meeting began to descend into chaos. People kept interrupting each other and Minister Campbell was struggling to keep order. Personal attacks on Pastor were now openly being made. People were saying that he is too strict and that love, mercy and compassion for someone who has fallen, should be the priority and that is what is expected from a good Pastor.

Deacon Hudson got to his feet and said that he is prepared to leave with many of the brethren and set up a new church. On hearing this, Pastor Ellington shouted "traitor" and there was a momentary hush across the meeting. "The church is going down Pastor and everybody knows it" Deacon Hudson shouted back.

Evangelist Harrison stood up and gave a full defence of the Pastor. Many people believe that he was ordained an Evangelist because he is white and Pastor saw this appointment as a means to draw more white people into his predominantly black church. A number of ambitious black brothers became resentful at his appointment and did not support him in his capacity of being the Men's Leader. This caused a great deal of frustration but he managed to overlook that and continue in his role as best he could.

Back and forth the meeting went with arguments and counter arguments until finally Pastor Ellington stood up to address the church. His abilities as a leader was now at a critical point. What he says now would affect the future direction, and possibly the very survival of the church.

"When the Lord called me to be the Pastor of this church I did not want to be" he began. "I tried to get out of that responsibility but couldn't. I knew that managing God's great people was an awesome responsibility and that a great many things went along with it – both good and bad. I do not consider this to be my church and I do not consider the growth from 26 people when we started out to over 5000 now, to be my achievement. It's the Lord that has been adding to this church and not my skills as Pastor. It's His church.

I have done my best by the grace of god for the last 18 years. I have laboured among you all and I have led you as I have been led by the Spirit of God. My record as Pastor is before you and you know my heart and my passion to see Christ fully formed in you all. I take nothing for myself. I do not draw a salary from the church. I work hard for the church as you all know, and my own children say that I put you before them. I admit that I sometimes do, because I love the church family.

Now it seems that many of you are turning your back on me. I have not done anything to any of you. What I have done is what any of you would do, and that is to make a decision as a parent in dealing with an issue in your home. I know you all love Jackie, and no one more than me and Mother Ellington, but I did not make Jackie wander outside of the church and pick up a sinner. I did not make her have a relationship with him and keep it all from her parents, her family and the church. It was not me who made her backslide. She was the one who made all these choices.

When I gave her a week to end the relationship, an ungodly relationship, she refused, and as hard as it was, I as Pastor of this church, could not allow her to carry on this lifestyle in my home and disobey our rules in this way. I may have been a bit hasty in asking her to leave but I think that I made the right decision. I am sorry that she lost the baby but people are talking as if I wanted it to happen and some are even suggesting that I may have pushed her down the stairs. That is simply not true. I love my daughter and would never do anything to hurt her.

If because of my stand on this matter, some of you choose to leave this church, then I will be hurt by it, but I will accept it. I want no strife and I want no conflict. This is the church of Jesus Christ and my fight is with the devil and not with any of you.

I am going to leave now. I shall be here again on Sunday to carry on with the service of the Lord. I will be standing in my post, regardless of how many are here standing with me. God bless you all."

A round of applause rang out as Pastor Ellington left the platform and walked through the middle of the congregation to his car outside. Mother Ellington followed him as did Dawn and David. As he started the car, Mother Ellington placed her hand on his and looked into his eyes. He stared back almost choking with emotion. She smiled momentarily, and he drove off.

Inside the church, the congregation continued to discuss what had just happened. Many were shocked at what they had heard and others were now confused about what to do. Minister Campbell asked everyone to go away and to consider what they had heard. "As for me and my house" he told the people, "we will serve the Lord at Mount Zion Refuge."

For the next few days, Jackie begins to come to terms with her miscarriage. She is still in the grieving process but is making plans for the future. Soon she will try again to have a child. For the moment, there is a wedding to organise. Many messages have been left on her mobile phone from her family but she has not responded to any of them.

On Saturday morning, there is a knock at the door and she peers out of the window to see who it is. To her surprise it is her father. She hesitates and then closes the curtains and goes back inside. She sits down on a chair. The door is knocked a few more times. She remains seated. In silence. Her father then leaves.

She has discussed the matter with Paul and though she does not hate her father, she does not wish to see him either. She is planning on making her own life with Paul. Soon she will start looking for a job and sorting out where she will live with Paul. The registry office has been booked for the wedding and it will be a quiet wedding with few people. She is trying to remain positive and to look ahead for better days.

Chapter 8

Sunday has now arrived and Pastor is in his study preparing his sermon as normal. He is a quite nervous because following the members meeting on Wednesday, he does not know how many people will be turning up for church. Since the meeting, the phone has not rang once. This is unusual because the phone is always ringing at Pastor's house. The silence is eerie.

Pastor Ellington is torn inside. He is feeling defeated but refuses to show it on the outside. For his family, for his ministry, he must show strength. He tells himself that he will not break down. He will not cry, no matter how much it hurts. "The Lord god is my strength" he says to himself quoting a verse of scripture.

If there are few people in church, how will he be able to preach? How will he be able to continue paying for the church building with the little offering that would be coming in? How would he feel when he meets brethren or Ministers from other churches? What would he say to them? Never mind all that, how can he reconnect with Jackie. He has just lost his grandchild and he feels bad about it all.

With all this going through his mind, how will he be able to preach his sermon? He begins to pray and to ask the Lord for strength.

Before they get into the car, Mother Ellington hugs him and says that everything will be alright, and that though some may leave, she will be going nowhere. "We will get through this as a family and we will get through this as a church" she reassures him with a kiss. "We are in this together."

On arrival at church, there seems a lot of empty spaces in the car park. Ignoring this, the Ellington family enter the church at the side entrance and Pastor goes into the Vestry to be alone. He remains in there praying and seeking the Lord. Singing is heard in the background. After a while, the sound of the singing grows louder and louder. This brings a smile to Pastor's face as he believes that many people are in church.

Before leaving the Vestry, he raises his hands to utter a final thanksgiving prayer and he makes his way along the corridor and enters the main hall on the platform. He sees a large crowd but notices that there are a lot of people missing. At least it's not the embarrassing turnout that he originally feared.

In looking around the platform, everyone was there except Deacon Hudson. Pastor is not surprised by this and feels that he must be busy setting up his own church by now. He was always ambitious and was the most resentful when he did not get the Assistant Pastor position when it became available.

Pastor thanked everyone for coming and said that the church will continue as before and be led by the Holy Spirit. "For all those that has left, for whatever reason, let us be brotherly when we meet them in the street and in the supermarket. Let there be no animosity. No ill-feeling. No conflict. For we are brethren."

He then began his sermon on love. In times of peace he prepares the people for war. In times of war he preaches healing and peace. This philosophy has stood him in good stead in the past and it will work for him now.

A few weeks later, Jackie has found another marketing role and has started working. Her mother has been to visit her a few times and is getting on really well with Paul. Dawn and David have also been in touch and they are all intending to be at the wedding. A number of the brethren have also been invited and have agreed to come.

Mother Ellington has been speaking with Jackie to come back to church but she refuses. Her mother says that she should not forget the Lord and that she must continue to serve Him. "If you do not feel that you can come to Mount Zion Refuge" she tells her daughter, "then find another church where they believe in the Bible, and go there, but you must go somewhere. The salvation of your soul is precious.

It's no point gaining the whole world if you lose your soul."

Jackie tells her mother that she wants to get back to church but Paul will not go as he feels that all christians are hypocrites. They discuss it and Jackie confesses that it is because he blames dad for the miscarriage. She tells Jackie that her father really wants to see her but she says that she cannot see him. "I am with Paul now, and if dad sees me, he must see Paul also. He is part of my life now and we are together. We come as a pair."

Mother Ellington understands Jackie's point of view and is hoping beyond hope that somehow the situation will change. There is now seven weeks to the wedding and something has got to give.

It is ten past five in the afternoon and Pastor Ellington is getting into his car as he finishes work. A mechanic by trade, he has successfully built up his garage business to the point where it almost runs itself. He has good workers under him and he is able to simply monitor what is happening and keep an eye on cash flow. He sees this business as a necessary task that finances him and allows him to be almost full time in the ministry. If he were to give it up, then he would need to take a salary from the church, and this is something that he does not want to do.

On most days he works perhaps two to three hours and the rest he uses to visit brethren in their homes to pray with them, to give counsel, or to settle matters. With over 5000 people (less than that now) he is always busy.

He signals to a fellow worker and tells him that he will see him tomorrow at about noon. With that he drives away and heads for home. Tonight he has a meeting with a rather distressed brother who called him to say that he is depressed. Apparently, this brother has been out of work for six weeks and since he heard one Minister say that if a man does not work, neither shall he eat, he has been feeling ashamed and worthless. Pastor assured him that the Minister was not talking about him personally but was simply quoting the scripture. Nevertheless he would come round that evening to talk to him.

After that, Pastor is off to see the parents of a teenage child who is playing up and getting into all sorts of mischief with a bad crowd. His parents have tried everything and they are at the end of their patience and do not know what to do. They bailed him out of the police station for shoplifting this morning and have asked Pastor to intervene.

Pastor thinks that he had better get some food before going to his two appointments in the evening. Whilst stationary at a set of traffic lights, he had his head down and was looking into the glove compartment to find one of his favourite CD's. Whilst doing so, a car crashed into the front right hand side of his vehicle and swung it across the road violently. Steam was coming out of the wrecked car. Blood was streaming down his face. Onlookers rushed around the car, opened the door and found Pastor unconscious.

An ambulance was called and it took him to hospital. Two hours has past and Pastor Ellington is slowly coming out of unconsciousness. His eyes are blurry. There is a sharp pain in his neck. "Ruth. Ruth" he mumbles referring to his wife. "I am here darling. I am here" a voice replies. Pastor opens his eyes and now has focus. He looks around and realises that he is in hospital. Mother Ellington is at his bedside with a nurse who is checking some monitors with instruments that runs to his arm.

"What happened?" Pastor says weakly.
"You have been in a car accident"
"I didn't have an accident. Oh, but I remember something hit my car and I have woken up here."
"Yes you were unconscious. The doctors are still running tests but they say that you are going to be fine."
Outside the room Dawn and David are waiting. Joel is also there with his girlfriend Eve and their two year old son Ramone. No one is speaking. They all look worried. Ramone is walking up and down and playing with a toy. Eve is patrolling the area as Ramone keeps walking away to explore.

The door opens and Mrs Ellington comes out. She tells everybody that their father has come to and that he will be alright. A huge sigh of relief is heard and the children go inside for the one minute that they are allowed to see their father. Everyone hugs him except for Joel who keeps his distance. He is concerned about his father and is pleased that he seems alright. But he won't get sentimental, and he won't show any emotion. He is still angry with his father.

The nurse apologises but says that everybody must leave so that he can get his rest. Left alone, Pastor is thinking about Jackie. She did not come to see him. Maybe she does not care. Maybe he has lost her for good, he thinks to himself. He has called her but she has not answered the phone. He has visited but either she was not in or she did not want to answer the door to him. She seems to be home when other members of the family go round but she seems never there when he has visited. I can take a hint he says, but he cannot bear to live with that situation. He must get back into her life somehow. But how? He begins to cry. Sounds of sobbing can be heard coming from his room. Still sedated, he drifts off to sleep.

The next morning he is told that he will be able to go home that afternoon. His wife is coming to collect him at 3 O'clock and he passes the time staring at the ceiling and contemplating the future. At lunchtime, he drifts off to sleep again. A short while after, he becomes aware that someone is holding his hand. He opens his eyes and sees Jackie.

"Oh my god" he says.
"No it's not god, it's only me"

Jackie replies with a smile.

"I didn't think that you would come"

"You are still my father and I still love you"

"I am so sorry about the baby"

"Me too, but what's done is done. I don't blame you. It was me that fell down the stairs."

"Yes but it was me that made you cry and run away."

The two speak for a while. Pastor asks Jackie to come round to the house, but she says that Paul won't come there because he does not accept him. Pastor assures her that he has nothing against Paul and that he is only against the relationship because it is outside of god's will. Jackie gets up to leave and is asked not to go yet. She declines and says that the situation has not changed, and therefore she must go. He calls out to her but she closes the door and leaves disappointed.

A week later, Pastor, now back on his feet, is in the church office with Brother Michael and Sister Janice. Elder Samuels is also present. Michael and Janice went to London together for three days and stayed in the same hotel. They are both single and everyone knows that they are good friends. Rumours began to spread about them. They deny any wrong doing and say that they only went there to see what London was like. They say that they stayed in separate bedrooms and that nothing of a sexual nature occurred.

With no way of proving otherwise, Pastor told them that because they did not tell anyone before they went and that it looked as if they went away in secret, that this would automatically give rise to rumours of a dirty weekend. He also said that they had placed themselves in a vulnerable position because the flesh is given the opportunity to rise up and that is always a mistake.

Brother Michael argued that carnal people will always think carnal thoughts but he knew that nothing happened.

"Sister Janice and I are just friends and what is the problem of friends hanging out together or going on a trip together. We are supposed to be neither male nor female but one in Christ. She is my sister. Tongue talking waste of time people can take a running jump" said Michael angrily.

"Brother Michael" said Elder Samuels, "you are the one responsible for this situation, both you and Sister Janice. Your very actions have given rise to your honesty and integrity being called into question. A man and a woman going off together, in secret, out of town, and booking into the same hotel for a few days. This does look suspicious. Even if people think that nothing happened, they would still have an element of doubt. You should give no place to the devil and you should abstain from the very appearance of evil. Not that you did anything wrong, but you must stay away from the very appearance of it."

"I can see that now Elder" declared Sister Janice. "Going away together was a mistake. I am sorry."

"How about you Brother Michael?" asked Pastor.
"Well, I still can't see that I did anything wrong. It's a shame that a brother cannot spend time with a friend if the friend is of the opposite sex. It's a shame."

The meeting continued for another half an hour before it was closed in prayer. Brother Michael left disappointed and angry at the whole situation. He resents having to be called before the Ministers to explain an innocent trip because some carnal minded people were talking. If he knew who they were he would give them a piece of his mind. He feels that he cannot stay and worship with a bunch of people like these and he decides on his way home, that he will not be coming back to this church.

On Sunday morning, Pastor Ellington announced that Gordon Brown, the Prime Minister, and his wife, was coming to Mount Zion Refuge the following Sunday. The congregation cheered.

"An official from 10 Downing Street called me two days ago" he explained, "and asked if the Prime Minister could make a visit. Of course I said yes. There will be a number of officials with him as well as secret service officers, and television cameras. We are absolutely delighted that he has chosen Mount Zion Refuge and we will do our best to make our guests feel welcome."

For the rest of the week, Pastor and a small team that he formed as an organising committee, worked hard on what would be required on Sunday. They were sent a list by Number 10 of protocols to be followed, and secret service officers visited to discuss security matters. The police also came as did some reporters to check out positioning for their TV cameras.

The whole church was excited. After a testing time in recent months, this was a welcome diversion and one that would generate a great deal of publicity for the church.

When the big day arrived, Pastor and a dozen chosen people arrived early. They each had a checklist of things to do before the masses would arrive. Pastor was nervous. He had not been on television before and he spent a lot of time on his sermon, to get it just right.

As he looked around the main hall where the service was to be held, Mother Ellington came in hurriedly with a worried look on her face.
"Joseph, I have just had a call from Jackie. She is leaving."
"Leaving. Going where?"
"She is leaving for good. She is moving to Birmingham this morning. She called from the station to say goodbye."

Pastor thought for a moment. "I am going to get her" he said and ran through the church, got into his car and drove off at speed. The service was due to start in one hour. The television cameras were being set up in their positions, sound checks were being made, policemen with dogs were outside discussing strategy. And the Pastor has driven off into the distance.

As he was driving to the railway station, a journey of some twenty minutes, he was pleading with the Lord for him not to miss the train. He wanted to see Jackie before she left. On arrival, Pastor ran into the station looking desperately on the notice boards to see which platform the train to Birmingham was leaving from. On finding it, he ran down the stairs and through the barriers, looking desperately through carriage windows as fast as he could. The train was due to leave in ten minutes.

Finally he saw Jackie and Paul seated. He jumped on board and startled them.

"Jackie please don't leave" he said. "I realise now that I was wrong. I was selfish and I was thinking about myself and not what was best for you. I know now that you and Paul are in love and that I must accept that. I have come to tell you that I do accept you both and to ask for your forgiveness."

"It's too late" replied Paul. "It's because of you that we are going"

"I know, I know. Please, I am begging you. Paul, I never gave you a chance. I should have treated you better. I was foolish. I didn't want my daughter to marry a white person and because you are not a christian. But I realise now that I cannot stand in the way of true love and it would be wrong of me to do so."

"Dad, why did you not say any of this before?" asked Jackie in tears.

"Because I was stubborn. I realise that now, and I can't bear the thought of you being out of my life. I love you so much."

"Your tickets please" said a voice behind them. It was the Guard checking tickets before the train leaves the station.

"I am sorry dad, we have to go"

"Won't you reconsider? Please"

"No. We have made plans," said Paul.

Feeling defeated, Pastor Ellington kisses Jackie and says goodbye. He stretches out his hand to Paul. Paul refuses to shake his hand and Pastor is asked by the Guard to leave as he has no ticket.

He stands outside of the carriage, looking at Jackie who is staring back at him in tears. Pastor is crying too. Paul is holding Jackie's hand to comfort her and does not look in Pastor's direction.

As the train pulls out of the station, Pastor drops to his knees in agony. He is pained for his loss. He stays there for five minutes sobbing, before getting up, and walking slowly to his car.

As he sat down in his car, he began to think about all the happy years that he had with Jackie and how it all may be gone for good. Eventually, he started the engine and drove off. Forty minutes later, he arrived at the home of Joel his eldest son. Joel was shocked to see him and asked him what he was doing there when it was in the middle of church time. Pastor Ellington poured his heart out to Joel and asked for forgiveness for being a bad father. Joel told him that he was not a bad father, it was just that he prioritised the church over his family and that it was hard growing up as a Pastor's son.

The two spoke openly and emotionally like they have never done before. They hugged. Paul said that he was sorry for all the things that he had said to him and that he did not mean them. He was just angry at the time.

The service back at Mount Zion Refuge was now over. Pastor had missed it. In his absence, which caused a great deal of panic, Minister Campbell, the Assistant Pastor, welcomed the Prime Minister and preached the sermon.

In the night service, Pastor Ellington apologised to the church for not being present in the morning but said that he had an emergency situation to deal with concerning Jackie. He told the congregation that she has left for a new life in Birmingham and that the church must pray for her.

The following Sunday morning was "family day", a day when believers would invite their loved ones to service and a special message was preached. Special songs were sung, four babies were dedicated to the Lord, and six couples came forward to recommit themselves to each other.

Pastor began to preach about the importance of family. Children are an heritage of the Lord he said and that the Lord knew what He was doing when He instituted the family. He cited many examples of families in the Bible, strong ones, and ones that had problems. He mentioned Jacob's house and the jealousy that existed against Joseph. He mentioned Cain and Abel which led to murder in the family, and he cited what happened with King David and his children.

As he was preaching, the doors opened at the back of the hall and in walked Jackie and Paul. This caused quite a stir among the people as Jackie had not been in church for many months. The couple sat down at the back. Pastor Ellington could not believe his eyes. He wanted to run over to his daughter and give her a huge bear hug but he was in the middle of a sermon. "So we can see that in the Bible there are many examples of conflict and problems. This affects all families." He paused, and then looked in the direction of Jackie. "I have found out that being a father is a very difficult thing. I have made good decisions and bad decisions. Some decisions that I have made, I have regretted and some I have been ashamed of. I am asking the good Lord to make me a better father and a better husband so that my family can be knit together in love and become stronger. I am asking the Lord to put it into the hearts of those that I have offended, those that I have wronged, to find it in their hearts to forgive me. And I am asking the Lord to help me with my weaknesses, and allow me to love and to accept those that come into my family, and to embrace them with a pure heart.

As I stand here, I can see Jackie and Paul seated at the back. I want you both to know that I love you and that you are a part of my family." Pastor's eyes began to swell up with tears and he was unable to speak coherently. "I am going ..." he said and could not continue.

Mother Ellington came over to him, gave him a handkerchief and stood by his side. He hugged her and the church stood cheering and singing. Pastor closed his eyes as he leaned on his wife's neck, overcome with emotion. When he opened his eyes he saw Jackie and Paul standing next to him. Jackie was crying and Paul was looking emotional. He hugged them both. Many of the Ministers and the church gathered round them as they sang "bind us together Lord, bind us together Lord, with chords that cannot be broken."

"I didn't think that I would see you again" said Pastor to Jackie as she wiped the tears from his eyes.
"Joel told me how you came round to see him and how you talked, and that was the day that the Prime Minister came to church. You missed the whole service to come and find me."

"Yes. Nothing else mattered. You were the only thing on my mind."

"I am touched that you did this for me dad. Paul and I have talked it over and we have decided to move back here."

The noise in the church was deafening. People were singing and dancing with joy.

The day is the 15th January 2008. Jackie is standing in her wedding dress next to Paul in the Registry Office. A proud Pastor Ellington has just given her away and the couple are saying their marriage vows. "By the powers invested in me, I now declare you man and wife" says the Registrar. "You may now kiss the bride." Paul does so and the audience claps and cheers. A few wolf whistles are heard.

At the Reception, Pastor is giving his speech. He tells of how he has grown to love Paul after a rocky beginning, but that now he feels very happy and proud to call him his son-in-law. He speaks of his love for Jackie and thanks the Lord that she has recommitted herself to god and has been singing wonderfully again in the choir.

Other brethren, family members and well wishers also give their speeches, and finally the Groom is called to say a few words. He says that he is the luckiest man in the world because after losing his father as a young child and his mother last year, that Jackie has been everything to him and that his life is only meaningful with her at his side. He declares his love for her and then says that he has two important announcements to make.

"The first announcement is that I want to get baptised." The crowd cheers loudly in surprise and excitement. Mother Ellington looks at Pastor and smiles, holding his hands.

"The second announcement" continued Paul, "is that … well, I think that I shall ask my wife to make it." He turns to Jackie, "Darling would you." Everyone begins to clap again and make noise.

"Well" says Jackie, "I am happy to say that, god willing, in September, I shall be bringing into the world, a very healthy baby." The noise of the applause and the people standing up and shouting for joy is deafening.

The End

A word from the Author

I hope that you have enjoyed reading this story, at least as much as I have enjoyed writing it. I am sure that you have found things common in the lives of many of the characters portrayed in the book, either in your own life or in the lives of many christians that you know.

The issue of finding love is an age old one and there seems to be a lack of proper teaching on the subject in many churches. Why this is the case is a matter of opinion, but there seems to be a reluctance by some Ministers to deal with the subject. They are confident and bold when teaching about one of the prophets, the life of Jesus or the early church, but when it comes to teaching about love, sex, courtship and marriage, they seem timid and uneasy.

This is unfortunate because these same Ministers will exhort the brethren not to "go to Egypt for help," but if they as the leaders do not provide the information in the church, where are the people to go when they are wrestling with these issues.

In my opinion, churches should do more to address our basic human needs of love, affection, dating, sex and marriage. It is not sufficient to simply tell people to fast and pray more. Practical things should be done by the church to deal with these issues.

The church needs to run teaching programmes on issues affecting believers who are single and these should cover topics such as how to go about finding a husband or wife, courtship, dating, how to survive singleness in a modern society, how to crucify the flesh, sanctification, and how to flourish as an individual and as a christian as a single person.

Equally, teaching should be on married life and how to get the best out of it, how to negotiate and handle disagreements, how to keep romance alive, how to raise children the Bible way, and other marital issues.

Loving on the Edge also raises issues about pastors who are so driven by "doing god's work" that they fail to spend enough time with their own families, who as a consequence, suffer for it in the long run, and sometimes may resent it. Many are virtually absentee fathers in the home because if they are not in church, they are out visiting other churches, or visiting their brethren, or in prayer meeting, Ministers meeting, or on the mission field, or doing something else "on god's business."

It is rare that you would see them actually sitting at home doing nothing, just relaxing with their families. They think that they must be on the go all the time, and I have seen that this leads to stress, fatigue, and physical and mental weariness.

A Pastor, man or woman, needs to spend quality time with their partner. Going to restaurants together.

Holding hands and strolling casually through the park. Taking a holiday or a weekend break together. Watching a movie whilst snuggling up under a blanket with drinks and snacks nearby, and the mobile phones switched off.

And as a parent, play with the kids, take them swimming, read them bed-time stories, take an interest in their school work, be there for them emotionally, spend quality time with them having fun and sharing life's experiences.

I strongly feel that Pastors are misleading themselves in thinking that they must be busy, busy, busy all the time, and they are missing out on real family life. I do not believe that the Lord wants his servants to neglect their families. I believe that He wants His Ministers to be good parents, good husbands or wives, and good role models in the church on how to live in the home.

Living a balanced life for me is very important. We should all strive for it, whether we are Ministers or not.

Finally, I want to acknowledge the fact that we are all human beings living in a body of flesh. Because of this, and not walking in the spirit, we can fall into temptation. If this happens, I do not believe that we should condemn the person, but we should help them to be restored in Christ.

Our aim is to get them to see their ways in the light of

god's Word, and for them to then make a change, through repentance, and fall in line with the Word.

Christians, through weakness or other reasons, can make wrong choices and we should not be like those who cast stones, criticize and condemn them, but be like Christ, who is compassionate, forgiving, and who lifts the soul.

In adulthood, we all do not have the same level of maturity. Likewise, in spiritual matters and in christian living, we all do not have the same level of maturity. Some people will behave badly and some will make wrong choices, but we are all in the race together, and when one falls, our duty is to help them to rise again, in the hope that we can all make it home together.

Lightning Source UK Ltd.
Milton Keynes UK
28 May 2010

154846UK00001B/42/P